力得文化
Leader Culture

MP3

英檢口說

10-60歲都適用的四週英語口說課！

高分術

常安陸 ◎ 著

- 是否每當心中燃起英語**學習動力**，卻被週遭的種種阻力迅速澆熄呢!?

  謎之聲：累+淚 Q_Q

- 是否每次想用英語勇於**表達思緒**，卻被莫名的...然後改口用了中文呢!?

  謎之聲：泣+殘念

- 是否每次看到週遭友人們閃耀奪目的**證照成績**，卻總是暗自在角落畫圈圈呢!?

  謎之聲：嘆息 +1

這不是老生常談，也不是在蓋你

由四大章節
【回答問題篇】、【簡短對話篇】、【簡短談話篇】和【申論篇】組成，題型精心規劃由基礎短句回答到段落申論回答，由淺而深故能更有效的學習，四週必能使你獲取英語口說高分。

高分真的不再遙不可及，而你也不用總是望洋興嘆 XDDD

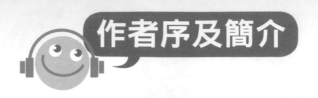
作者序及簡介

　　某較為嚴格的航空公司將空服人員的英語甄選標準設定為中高級以上亦即多益成績必須是 750 分以上才符合應徵資格。此航空公司曾聘用一位多益分數高達八百分以上的空姐但上班了半年後，卻發現她不僅外籍乘客的英語聽不懂，自己所能與乘客交談的內容也僅只是 "COFFEE? TEA?"，結果也引來一些輕佻的人在後面加上兩個字 "OR ME?" 來揶揄她（連起來就是「你要咖啡、茶、還是我？」），鬧得機艙裡又是訕笑又是尷尬。在座艙長的詢問之下才發現，她的分數都是補習班補出來的，補習班就是有一套讓人得分的高招，但是一到現實生活那些分數就不管用了。這位空服員所謂的八百多分就是早年只以聽與讀為主的測驗成績，現在多益加考了說與寫，但不像全民英檢必須聽說讀寫四項全合格才算一級通過。

　　類似空服員這樣考試成績與現實生活應用出現落差的情形，早年在赴美留學生中也很常見，許多傳統托福將近滿分（相當於英檢的高級）的學生，到了美國校園仍然聽不懂也說不出口，後來新托福改測聽說讀寫，也是由於發現只測聽與讀所產生的問題。而一次測完四項語言技能，似乎較符合語言的天性。

　　目前全民英檢測驗的順序是先測聽說再測讀寫，應試者在準備考試的過程中，須熟練應試技巧，但仍與實際情境產生脫節。學生在急於先通過聽與讀的考試壓力下，疏於練習說與寫，而且是在通過初試後一年內再找時間練習說與寫。這其實是違反人類語言生成天性的。當今英語教學泰斗道格拉斯・布朗 (H. Douglas Brown) 在聽力理解教學上特重互動 (Interaction)，特別是問答與會話這兩部份「在聽解過程中免不了會產生互動現象。會話特別與互動有密切關係，舉凡協商、澄清、引起注意、輪流，或是主題的提出、維持與結束，全都是互動的。考生即使熟練了應試技巧考了高分，終究還是難以把所學靈活運用在現實生活上。

　　因此編這本書的目的，除了希望能幫助急於要考英檢的學者，兼顧他在實際生活上的靈活運用，你第一眼看到的就是全真的試題，然後我們針對這些題目所提供的語料進行模擬問答、會話互動，再進一部分析這些語料的字彙、文法的運用，讓你一步一步都踏在真實考與用的情境中，既熟悉題型，又熟悉用法。

　　既然我們強調的是互動，就不能只是讀者與書的互動，而是隨著錄音檔中所引導的活動練習，先是機械式的練習困難的字彙語句，然後必須把學會的語句用在與真人的交談上，學習者可以二人結伴或三人以上編組，隨著書上設計的活動，自己另創造類似話題或文法句型的對話，把現實生活中可能面臨的難題拿出來與同伴一起解決，減少像前述空姐那樣的困境。

常安陸

編者序

　　口說其實是很多人避之不及的測驗之一，最主要的原因在於不敢開口以及不知道如何適切的表達，其實在透過階段性的訓練後，每個人都能於考場中有更佳的表現，而本書規劃了四週的口說訓練計劃，透過每天的練習(Day1~Day5)以及假日的複習(Day6~Day7)，循序漸進的方式訓練英語口語的表達，進而逐步克服考生心中的心理障礙，敢於表達自己，並透過這些訓練最後融入自己本身的答案，於考場中適切表達出自己的想法，獲取理想的成績。

力得文化編輯群

10-60 歲都適用的四週英語口說課！

一學就會的英檢口說高分術

目 次

WEEK ① 回答問題篇

Day 1	Monday	8
Day 2	Tuesday	16
Day 3	Wednesday	34
Day 4	Thursday	46
Day 5	Friday	54

WEEK ② 簡短對話篇

Day 1	Monday	68
Day 2	Tuesday	86
Day 3	Wednesday	98
Day 4	Thursday	110
Day 5	Friday	120

WEEK ③ 簡短談話篇

Day 1	Monday	128
Day 2	Tuesday	138
Day 3	Wednesday	150
Day 4	Thursday	160
Day 5	Friday	172

WEEK 4 申論篇

Day 1	Monday	188
Day 2	Tuesday	200
Day 3	Wednesday	204
Day 4	Thursday	214
Day 5	Friday	234

附錄

SCRIPT

Week 1 【回答問題篇】錄音稿

【Day 1-5】 243

Week 2 【簡短對話篇】錄音稿

【Day 1-5】 262

Week 3 【簡短談話篇】錄音稿

【Day 1-5】 282

Week 4 【申論篇】錄音稿

【Day 1-5】 307

一學就會的英檢口說高分術

	Week 1	Week 2	Week 3	Week 4
Day 1				
Day 2				
Day 3				
Day 4				
Day 5				
Day 6	review	review	review	review
Day 7	review	review	review	review

WEEK **1**

回答問題篇

WEEK 1 回答問題篇

DAY 1 MONDAY

　　本篇以口說的「回答問題」測驗作暖身，從模仿進一步直接應答問題了。現在先模擬一次全民英檢的口說「回答問題」測驗，考驗自己的回答能力，之後再就其他需要延伸與加強的能力練習。

　　回答問題的前提自然是必須完全聽得懂問題，所以必須先通過了聽力測驗之後，才適合做問答的測驗。不論大家是否已經通過了聽力測驗，口說的回答要領其實與聽力問答測驗是一樣的。熟習了聽力技巧也就準備好口說問答了。我們回顧一下全民英檢的聽力基本技巧，常見的類型有 Yes / No 和 Wh- 類的問題。如果他是以 Be 動詞或其他助動詞引導的問題，就必然是 Yes / No 類的問題，須以 Be 動詞或該助動詞回答。如果他是以 Wh- 疑問詞引導的問題，就必然是Wh- 類的問題，須以該相關疑問詞回答。句型舉例如下：

Be 動詞	問句	回答 (Yes / No)
Am, are, is / was, were	（依序）+ I, you, he / she, we / you / they...?	Yes, I, you, he / she, we / you / they + Be 動詞 No, 上述主詞 + 上述 Be 動詞 + not
助動詞	問句	回答
Do, does, did, can, have, ...	（依序）+ I, you, he / she, we / you / they...?	Yes, I, you, he / she, we / you / they + 助動詞 No, 上述主詞 + 上述助動詞 + not

Yes / no 問句	
Be 動詞問句	回答參考
Are you a student?	Yes, I **am** a student.
Was he a teacher?	No, he **was** not a teacher.
Were they all Chinese?	Yes, they **were** all Chinese.
Is this mine?	No, this **is** not yours.
助動詞問句	回答參考
Can she sing?	Yes, she **can** sing.
Will I see you tomorrow?	No, you **will** not see me tomorrow.
Has he eaten?	Yes, he **has**.
Did he stay	No, he **didn't**.
Would you fax it to me?	Of course I **would**.
Could she be the winner?	No, she **couldn't**.
Should we go now?	Certainly.
Wh- 問句 （此類問題最重要的是要聽清楚其開頭的第一個 wh- 字）	
What 問什麼	回答參考
What is your favorite color?	My favorite color is blue.
Where 問地點	回答參考
Where am I?	You are in Taiwan.
When 問時間	回答參考
When is the museum open?	It is open at 8 a.m.

Why 問理由	回答參考
Why is he late?	He missed the bus.
Who 問誰	回答參考
Who is he?	He is my father.
How 問如何	回答參考
How are you?	I am fine. Thank you.

上表中，How 的用法還有許多不同功能。

如問功能：How did / do you make it?

問量的多少：How many / much are / is they / it?

問時間：How long did you live here? How often do you excise?

問距離：How far is it from here?

Wh 問句還有一個重要的回答要領，就是聽清楚問句中的關鍵字（不包含那些疑問字），如 How much money do you have to buy the car? 關鍵字是 "money" 然後立即重述關鍵字來回答問題：I have 1,000,000 NTD.

以下找同伴一問一答再練習幾句：

What is your **favorite place to spend free time**?

My favorite place to spend free time is the park in my neighborhood.

How old were you **when you first went abroad**?

I **first went abroad when** I was twenty-two.

What are some places **we shouldn't smoke** ?
We shouldn't smoke in any public places.

How often do you **cut your hair**?
I **cut my hair** every month.

How **long** does **it take** to the MRT station?
It takes 10 minutes to the MRT station.

What kinds of pet do **you like** the most?
I like dog the most.

　　在測驗前，再回顧英檢口說的測驗標準，第二章我們做朗讀練習時偏重於發音的評分，此章則偏重語法、字彙的評分。

級分	分數	說明
5	100	發音清晰、正確，語調正確、自然；對應內容切題，表達流暢；語法、字彙使用自如，雖仍偶有錯誤，但無礙溝通。
4	80	發音大致清晰、正確，語調大致正確、自然；對應內容切題，語法、字彙之使用雖有錯誤，但無礙溝通。
3	60	發音、語調時有錯誤，因而影響聽者對其語意的瞭解。已能掌握基本句型結構，語法仍有錯誤；且因字彙、片語有限，阻礙表達。

2	40	發音、語調錯誤均多，朗讀時常因缺乏辨識能力而略過不讀；因語法、字彙常有錯誤，而無法進行有效的溝通。
1	20	發音、語調錯誤多且嚴重，又因語法錯誤甚多，認識之單字片語有限，無法清楚表達，幾乎無溝通能力。
0	0	未答 / 等同未答。

根據上述標準我們可以更精準的掌握答題的重點。下面就做一回口說測驗的 II. 回答問題

這個部分共有 10 題。題目已事先錄音，每題經由耳機播出二次，不印在試題冊上。第 1 至 5 題，每題回答時間 15 秒；第 6 至 10 題，每題回答時間 30 秒。每題播出後，請立即回答。回答時，不一定要用完整的句子，但請在作答時間內儘量的表達。

現在並按每題播出後 15 秒與 30 秒的時限作答，作答後最好把自己的答案寫下來，一者可以順便練習寫作，再者可以參考答案對照，看看有無用字、結構與文法上的錯誤。

請聽錄音 🎧 Mp3 001

Question 1: What is he doing right now?

（**15 秒**）

Question 2: What is your favorite place to spend free time? Why?

（**15 秒**）

Question 3: How old were you when you first went abroad? Why?

（**15** 秒）

Question 4: In some places we shouldn't smoke. What are some of these places?

（**15** 秒）

Question 5: What would you do if the fire alarm set off while you were watching a movie?

（**15** 秒）

Question 6: Do you feel more energetic in the morning, the afternoon, or the evening? Why?

（**30** 秒）

Question 7: Why do some people say that it isn't good to eat out nowadays? What do you think?

（**30** 秒）

Question 8: Do you feel happy easily? What might be some good ways to be happy?

（**30** 秒）

Question 9: Have you done something interesting last year? Tell me about it.

（**30** 秒）

Question 10: Would you rather travel to China or the U. S.? Why?

（**30** 秒）

參考答案

1.	a. He's eating lunch. b. He's taking a bus.
2.	a. I like to go to 228 Memorial Park because trees and flowers are beautiful. b. I like to go to Chiang Kai-shek Memorial Hall because it has the best theater in the city.
3.	a. I first went abroad when I was twenty-two. I went to the States to study. b. The first time I went abroad was when I twelve to learn English in England.
4.	a. We shouldn't smoke in any public places. b. We shouldn't smoke at any places with No-Smoking signs.
5.	a. I would rush to the exit immediately. b. I would stay seated and wait for the instruction to leave orderly.
6.	a. In the morning, because I usually sleep early and well. b. In the evening, because I am really relaxed after work.
7.	a. Sanitation of foods is the main concern for most people, and because of the tented oil problems nowadays, some people think it might not be a good idea to eat out. I think it's a loophole in the food security standards. b. People are afraid of the problematic food sources; even the famous fast food chain used the expired food supplier.

8.	a. Yes, I do feel happy easily. My way to be happy is to be content at all the time. when you sleep well, eat well, or get along with people well, it's kind of fun. b. No, I don't feel happy easily. My way to be happy is trying to be in other's shoes and find out why they don't like me.
9.	a. Yeah, I traveled to California. I visited Universal Studios to see how movies are produced and it was a lot of fun. b. Yes, I volunteered to teach English in the remote villages of TaiDong county. I found teaching those children is so meaningful to me.
10.	a. I would rather travel to China because the language, food, and customs are all suitable for my tastes. b. I would rather travel to the States because I want to learn English in an authentic language surrounding.

DAY ② TUESDAY

做完上一節，不知大家是否把自己模擬回答的答案寫下來，與參考答案對照了呢？如果發現答案不同，又如何得知自己的答案是否用字、結構與文法上正確呢？而現在就必須帶大家面對最根本的問題了，五大句型為最根本的基礎而這時就該用五大句型分析，至於用字與文法方面，我們在練習聽與說的同時，必然也會閱讀甚至練習寫作，這些都是增進聽說能力的基礎。千萬不要認為只是練習聽說，那聽說能力就會進步。必須認清聽說讀寫是一體不能偏廢的能力。例如下面我們就要教大家確認自己所回答得是否正確，就必須寫下自己的答案，然後用文法與結構的能力來自我檢查才行。

這個檢查所用的文法與結構能力以動詞時態、動詞五大句型、和句子構造為重點，這一節我們先溫故知新以五大句型來檢查句子的元素，用上節練習的參考答案作範例。不過我們不必逐句再分析，而是以五大句型的動詞特性，針對屬於該類動詞特性的句子解析。

五種單句的基本句型：
1. S+V（主詞＋動詞）
2. S+V+SC（主詞＋動詞＋主詞補語）
3. S+V+O（主詞＋動詞＋受詞）
4. S+V+O+OC（主詞＋動詞＋受詞＋受詞補語）
5. S+V+IO+DO（主詞＋動詞＋直接受詞＋間接受詞）
＊S：主詞　V：動詞　O：受詞　C：補語
　IO：直接受詞　DO：間接受詞

一、完全不及物動詞

Complete Intransitive Verb，不及物動詞縮寫為 **Vi**。

We shouldn't smoke in any public places.
S   Vi

我們不應該在任何公共場所吸煙。

I usually sleep early and well. 我通常睡得早，睡得好。
S   Vi

They fear for food security. 他們擔心的食品安全。
  S Vi

I traveled to California. 我們去了加利福尼亞。
S Vi

I volunteered to teach English. 我自願去教英語。
S Vi

　　以上各句除了主詞與動詞外，就沒有其他要素了。也就是說，除了形容詞、副詞及形容詞片語、副詞片語之外，沒有任何受詞或補語這就是完全不及物動詞。如第一句 in any public places 是副詞片語，修飾 smoke。

　　第二句 usually、early and well 都是副詞，修飾 sleep。第三句 for food security 也是副詞，修飾 fear。第四句 to California 也是副詞片語，修飾 traveled。第五句 to teach English 是不定詞當副詞，修飾 volunteered。

二、不完全不及物動詞

Complete Intransitive Verb，不及物動詞縮寫為 **Vt**。

I was twenty-two.
S Vi   SC

我曾經二十歲。

People are afraid of the problematic food sources.
  S   Vi   SC

人們害怕問題食物的來源。

I don't feel happy easily.
S   Vi   SC

我不易感到快樂。

The language, food, and customs are all suitable for my tastes.
          S   Vi   SC

語言、食物和習俗都和我味口。

　　不完全不及物動詞本身無法表達一個完全的意念，必須補上另一個名詞或形容詞才能成句。例如第一句 I was 「我是」我們一定要問「是甚麼」所以必須補上名詞 twenty-two 才能表達「我是 22 歲」。第二句 People are「人們是」必須補上 afraid 「害怕的」才能成句，而 of the problematic food sources 「有問題的食物來源」是副詞片語，修飾 afraid。第三句 I don't feel 「我不覺得」，必須補上 happy「快樂」才能成句，而 easily 是副詞，修飾 feel。第四句與第一句一樣 Be 動詞需補上形容詞 suit「適合的」才能成句，而 for my tastes 是副詞片語修飾 suit。這些補語因之稱為「主詞補語」(Subject Complement)。

三、完全及物動詞

Complete Transitive Verb，及物動詞縮寫為 **Vt**。

He's eating lunch.
S   Vt   O

他正在吃午餐。

He's taking a bus.
S   Vt   O

他正搭乘一輛公共汽車。

I would keep sitting on my seat.
S   Vt   O

我會繼續坐在我的座位上。

I like to go to Yangmingshan National Park.
S Vt   O

我喜歡去陽明山國家公園。

完全及物動詞完全不需要補語，但一定有受詞。從上面的句子可以看出來，只要有受詞這句子的意思就夠清楚了，其他字就都只是修飾語了。如第四句的 to Yangmingshan National Park 就是一個副詞修飾 go 而已。

四、不完全及物動詞

Incomplete Transitive Verb

They asked us not to smoke inside.
　S　　Vt　O　　　　OC

他們要求我們不要抽煙。

The police officer ordered the thief to drop the gun.
　　　　　　S　　　Vt　　　　O　　　OC

員警命令那個小偷，把槍放下。

He made his parents happy.
S　Vt　　　O　　OC

他使他的父母高興。

不完全及物動詞含有使動的作用，是一種作為動詞 (Factitive Verb)，上例句中的 to smoke, to drop the gun, happy 等，都是前面動詞作為的結果。to smoke, to drop the gun, 是不定詞片語作為補語，happy 則是形容詞作為補語。

五、使用兩個受詞的動詞「直接受詞」Direct Verb, 縮寫為 DO，「間接受詞」Indirect Verb, 縮寫為 IO，又稱為授與動詞 Dative Verb。

<u>(You)</u> <u>Give</u> <u>me</u> the <u>book</u>.
  S   Vt   IO   DO

給我那本書。

<u>She</u> <u>read</u> the <u>boy</u> a bed time <u>story</u>.
 S   Vt   IO   DO

她給小男孩讀了床邊故事。

<u>He</u> just <u>told</u> <u>me</u> the <u>news</u>.
 S   Vt   IO   DO

他剛告訴我消息。

　　授與動詞是由「受人以物」(give a person something) 的基本觀念產生的。這個「人」與「物」都是句子中的受詞，所以就有了兩個受詞了。通常人是間接受詞，物是直接動詞，因為真正給的是物，接受那物的才是人。

　　若希望自己造的句子符合句型的結構，最好的辦法就是用這五種句型來練習翻譯：

一、完全不及物動詞

　　1. 春風化雪

　　＿＿＿＿＿＿＿＿＿＿＿＿＿＿＿＿＿＿＿＿＿＿＿

　　2. 靜水流深（大智若愚）

　　＿＿＿＿＿＿＿＿＿＿＿＿＿＿＿＿＿＿＿＿＿＿＿

　　3. 天亮了

　　＿＿＿＿＿＿＿＿＿＿＿＿＿＿＿＿＿＿＿＿＿＿＿

　　4. 分秒必爭

　　＿＿＿＿＿＿＿＿＿＿＿＿＿＿＿＿＿＿＿＿＿＿＿

　　5. 食物不新鮮

　　＿＿＿＿＿＿＿＿＿＿＿＿＿＿＿＿＿＿＿＿＿＿＿

　　6. 他不適應

　　＿＿＿＿＿＿＿＿＿＿＿＿＿＿＿＿＿＿＿＿＿＿＿

　　7. 那工作不合算

　　＿＿＿＿＿＿＿＿＿＿＿＿＿＿＿＿＿＿＿＿＿＿＿

　　8. 看情形而定

　　＿＿＿＿＿＿＿＿＿＿＿＿＿＿＿＿＿＿＿＿＿＿＿

　　9. 我可能很快回來

　　＿＿＿＿＿＿＿＿＿＿＿＿＿＿＿＿＿＿＿＿＿＿＿

　　10. 他明天出國

　　＿＿＿＿＿＿＿＿＿＿＿＿＿＿＿＿＿＿＿＿＿＿＿

一、完全不及物動詞 參考答案請聽錄音後複誦 🎧 **Mp3 002**

   1. The snow melts away in spring.

   2. Still water runs deep.

   3. Day breaks. Day dawned. It breaks.

   4. Every minute counts.

   5. The food can't keep.

   6. He doesn't fit in.

   7. The work doesn't pay.

   8. It depends.

   9. I may return very soon.

  10. He goes abroad tomorrow.

二、不完全不及物動詞

1. 眼見為憑

_____

2. 他顯得很高興

_____

3. 他似乎很天真

_____

4. 街道似乎很髒亂

_____

5. 不要讓他看似一個乞丐

_____

6. 他保持沈默

_____

7. 請保持安靜

_____

8. 奮鬥後，他變富有了

_____

9. 他變高興了

_____

10. 他的臉色發紅

_____

二、不完全不及物動詞 參考答案請聽錄音後複誦 🔊 **Mp3 003**

1. Seeing is believing.

2. He looks very happy.

3. He seems naïve.

4. The streets appeared messy.

5. Don't make him appear a beggar.

6. He remained silent.

7. Please keep quiet.

8. After the struggle, he became rich.

9. He went happy.

10. His face turned blushed.

三、完全及物動詞

1. 我喜歡他

   _____

2. 他們需要愛

   _____

3. 他們想要去游泳

   _____

4. 他認為那電影很棒

   _____

5. 他喜歡跟女孩說話

   _____

6. 我們忍不住笑了

   _____

7. 雖然天氣很熱，我不介意關窗

   _____

8. 那公司正在考慮改變政策

   _____

9. 我們靠希望而生存

   _____

10. 衣食足而後知禮義

   _____

11. 要開始下雨了（原來沒下，後來才下）

   _____

12. 下雨了（既然開始下了，不再是不確定）

   _____

三、完全及物動詞 參考答案請聽錄音後複誦 🎧 Mp3 004

1. I like him.

2. They need love.

3. They want to go swimming.

4. He thinks that the movie is good.

5. He enjoys talking to girls.

6. We cannot help laughing.

7. I don't mind closing the window though it's very hot.

8. The company is considering changing the policy

9. Hope keeps us alive.

10. Wealth enables men to be courteous.

11. It started to rain.

12. It started raining.

四、不完全及物動詞

1. 老師要求這小女孩站起來

   _____

2. 當我走進來時聽見他正在唱歌

   _____

3. 我們選湯姆為代表

   _____

4. 我們選他做領導

   _____

5. 他們使他成為戰士

   _____

6. 我們稱他為民國之父

   _____

7. 他雙親稱他湯姆

   _____

8. 我覺得這是一部有趣的電影

   _____

9. 我相信他是一個好老師

   _____

10. 保持你的嘴閉著

    _____

11. 請讓自己感覺自在

    _____

四、不完全及物動詞 參考答案請聽錄音後複誦 🎧 Mp3 005

1. The teacher asked the little girl to stand up.

2. I heard him singing when I walked in.

3. We elected Tom to be representative.

4. We chose him leader.

5. They made him a warrier.

6. We call him "The Father of the Republic."

7. His parents named him Tom.

8. I found it a very interesting movie.

9. I believe that he is a good teacher.

10. Keep your mouth shot.

11. Please make yourself at home.

【Day 2】
Tuesday

五、授與動詞

1. 凱文給我一支筆

   _____

2. 蘇借一本書給我

   _____

3. 他買一張地圖給我

   _____

4. 我發電郵給我的朋友

   _____

5. 他提供我大量資訊

   _____

6. 她讀一些有名的文章給我聽

   _____

7. 我可以幫她找到遺失的鑽石

   _____

8. 我女友做派給我吃

   _____

9. 我問他一個問題

   _____

10. 他對我開一個玩笑

    _____

11. 他對我使出詭計

    _____

12. 我不懷恨他

    _____

13. 他把石塊扔向那隻貓

_____

14. 他扔給那隻狗一根骨頭

_____

五、授與動詞 參考答案請聽錄音後複誦 🔊 Mp3 006

1. Kevin gave me a pen.

2. Sue lent me a book.

3. He bought me a map.

4. I forward my friends an e-mail.

5. He offer me lots of information.

6. She read me some famous articles.

7. I can find her the lost diamond.

8. My girlfriend made me a pie.

9. I asked him a question.

10. He told me a joke.

11. He did a trick to us.

12. I hold a grudge against him.

13. He threw the cat a stone. = He threw a stone at the cat.

14. He threw the dog a bone. = He threw a bone to the dog.

有時間接受詞移到直接受詞後面要家介系詞，但嚴格來說加了介系詞的名詞就不算動詞的受詞了，只能算是介系詞的受詞：

V+ 直受 + 介系詞 + 受（介詞因不同的動詞而有所不同）

V+ 物 +to+ 人：

give / lend / send / write / bring / hand / pass / deliver / show / teach / tell / sell

pay / owe / do / promise / offer / read / show / sing / take

V+ 物 +for+ 人：

Buy / bring / book / build / cook / fetch / find / keep / knit / order / reserve get

leave / make / do

V+ 物 +of+ 人： ask

V+ 物 +on+ 人： play（愚弄、使詭計）

　　通常間接受詞放在直接受詞之前，但有時為了加強語氣或使意義更明白，才會把間接受詞放後面，不過在文法上既然這個受詞前面有介系詞，就不再是授與動詞的受詞了，例句如下：

He gave me a pen. = He gave a pen to me.

He bought me a book. = He bought a book for me.

I need to ask you a favor. = I need to ask a favor of you.

He played us a mean trick = He played a mean trick on us.

　　授與動詞概分四類：授與 (give) 東西，告知 (tell) 事情，貢獻 (render) 服務，及施行 (perform) 恩惠。前三者都可以在間接受詞前加 to 改成介詞片語，為有第四類必須用 for 表目的：

Bring me some food. = Bring some food for me.

DAY ③ WEDNESDAY

做過了英檢口說測驗，我們也看看多益口說考試內容，首先看看測驗內容及評分方式。

	口說
測驗介紹	多益口說測驗是評量考生職場英語口說能力的測驗。專業評分人員給分之重點是考生的發音、語調、輕重緩急、文法、字彙，以及回答是否切題及完整。
測驗題數	六大題型共 11 題
測驗時間	20 分鐘
方　　式	網路化測驗
分數範圍	0 ～ 200 分 (以 10 分為級距)
能力等級	1 ～ 8 級
內　　容	Respond to questions 回答問題
題　　數	3
作　　答	15 秒 / 30 秒
準　　備	無
說　　明	依據題目設定的情境，回答與日常生活有關的問題
評分級距	0 ～ 3

評分指標

分數	回答情形
3	回答完整、符合問題和社交上的要求。 1. 聽者輕易可聽懂。 2. 詞彙的選擇適當。 3. 使用結構滿足題目的要求。
2	回答部分正確，但不能完整、適當、準確的回答問題。 1. 聽者需努力才可聽懂，但大多是明白易懂。 2. 雖然整體的意思很清楚，詞彙的選擇可能有限或某種程度上是不精確的。 3. 聽者需努力才可理解其語言結構。
1	回應無法有效回答問題。無法成功的傳達相關資訊。 1. 聽者無法完全聽懂。 2. 選擇詞彙可能不準確或需要重複的提示。 3. 無法完全理解其語言結構。
0	沒有回應或回應中不說英語，或回應與問題完全無關。

【Day 3】Wednesday

　　英檢回答問題的練習，與多益口說稍有不同。4-6 題會先設定一個情境，然後回答問題，7-9 題多了「用提供的資訊回答」，留待下節我們再練習。現在就以多益 4-6 題試做一遍。

指示將顯示在螢幕上,你會聽到錄音指示。然後第四題的介紹和問題會出現在螢幕上,並聽到錄音,接著聽到提示音「嗶」聲。就開始 15 秒的時間回答。

Questions 4–6: Respond to questions:

Directions: In this part of the test, you will answer three questions. For each question, begin responding immediately after you hear a beep. No preparation time is provided. You will have 15 seconds to respond to Questions 4 and 5, and 30 seconds to respond to Question 6.

問題 **4–6**:回答問題:

說明:在此部分,你將回答三個問題。聽到提示「嗶」音後開始回答每個問題。無額外的準備時間。你有 15 秒回答第 4 和 5 題, 30 秒的時間回答第 6 題。

TOEIC Speaking
Question 4-11

聽錄音  Mp3 007

Imagine that you are participating in a research study about allergy. You have agreed to answer some questions in a telephone interview.

What kinds of allergic symptoms do you, your family members have?

Response time: 15 seconds

【Day 3】
Wednesday

TOEIC Speaking
Question 5-11

聽錄音 Mp3 008

Imagine that you are participating in a research study about allergy. You have agreed to answer some questions in a telephone interview.

What kinds of allergic symptoms do you, your family members, or friends have?

Response time: 15 seconds

TOEIC Speaking
Question 6-11

聽錄音 Mp3 009

Imagine that you are participating in a research study about allergy. You have agreed to answer some questions in a telephone interview.

What allergens cause those symptoms of you, your friends, or your family members?

Response time: 30 seconds

參考答案

Question 04 聽錄音並複誦 Mp3 010

In summer, my <u>mother</u> <u>gets</u> <u>allergy</u> in air-condition rooms for a
S   Vt   O

long time. <u>I</u> usually <u>suffer</u> from allergy when seasons change.
S   Vi

My <u>father</u> <u>is</u> <u>allergic</u> to seafood and milk.
S   Vi   SC

Question 05 聽錄音並複誦 🎧 Mp3 011

My <u>mother</u> <u>gets</u> running <u>nose</u> because she stays in air-condition
　　　S　　Vt　　　　　O

rooms for too long. <u>I</u> usually <u>sneeze</u> and my respiratory <u>system</u>
　　　　　　　　　　S　　　　Vi　　　　　　　　S

<u>becomes</u> <u>uncomfortable</u> when seasons change. My father's <u>skin</u>
　Vi　　　　SC　　　　　　　　　　　　　　　　　　S

<u>rashes</u> when he eats seafood and milk.
　Vi

Question 06 聽錄音並複誦 🎧 Mp3 012

Air <u>pollution</u> and weather <u>cause</u> my allergic <u>reactions</u>.
　　　S　　　　　　　　Vt　　　　　　O

<u>Temperature</u> and moist change <u>are</u> my mother's <u>allergen</u>.
　　　　　　S　　　　　　　　Vi　　　　　SC

<u>Allergens</u> from particular foods <u>bring</u> my <u>father</u> some allergic
　S　　　　　　　　　　　　　　Vt　　IO

<u>reactions</u>.
　DO

　　上一節我們的文法結構重點是五大句型，這一節我們仍然再參考答案上在複習一次五大句型，不過這一節我們要加上另一個重點就是句子構造的種類，概分為單句 (simple sentence)、合句 (compound sentence)、以及複句 (complex sentence) 三種。

一、單句，就是一個句子中只包含一個主詞和一個動詞的，即以前述的答案為例：

My <u>mother</u> <u>gets</u> <u>allergy</u> staying in air-condition rooms for
　　　 S　　 Vt　　 O

too long. 我母親在空調的房間裡待太長時間會過敏。

My <u>father</u> <u>is</u> <u>allergic</u> to seafood and milk.
　　 S　　 Vi　 SC

我父親是對海鮮和牛奶過敏。

Air <u>pollution and weather</u> <u>cause</u> my allergic <u>problems</u>.
　　　　　　 S　　　　　 Vt　　　　　 O

空氣污染和天氣導致我過敏的問題。

<u>Temperature and moist change</u> <u>are</u> my mother's <u>allergen</u>.
　　　　　　 S　　　　　　　 Vi　　　　 SC

溫度和濕度的改變是我母親的過敏原。

<u>Allergens</u> from particular foods <u>bring</u> my <u>father</u> allergic
　 S　　　　　　　　　　　　 Vt　　 IO

<u>reactions</u>. 特定的食物過敏原帶來我爸爸的過敏反應。
　 DO

二、合句，是由兩個或兩個以上的獨立子句 (independent clause) 所構成的。子句與子句之間要用對等連詞 (coordinate conjunction)，區分為

㈠ 累積連詞：and, both... and, not only... but also, no less than, as well as, furthermore, besides, moreover。

㈡ 選擇連詞：or, either... or, nor, neither... nor, otherwise, or else。

㈢ 反意連詞：but, yet, while, nevertheless, still, however, whereas, only, notwithstanding。

㈣ 推論連詞：for, therefore, so, thus, hence, wherefore, consequently, accordingly 等。❶

前述的答案有：

I usually sneeze and my respiratory system becomes
S   Vi   S   Vi

uncomfortable. 我經常打噴嚏，我的呼吸系統也變得不舒服。
    SC

其他的例子：

The army remained silent, for they didn't want to alarm the enemy.

軍隊保持沉默，因為他們不想驚動敵人。

---

❶ 還有更多的解釋與例句，請參閱：錢歌川，翻譯的技巧 The Technique of Translation，台灣開明書局，台北，民國六十二年。

兩個單句 "The army remained silent" 與 "she didn't want to alarm the enemy." 藉由逗號（,）和對等連接詞 for 隔開而形成合句。

I made my promises ; She gets her gifts.

我實踐承諾；她獲取她的禮物。

兩個單句 I made my promises. 與 She gets her gifts. 藉由分號（;）隔開而構成合句。

The audience was very excited, so I stayed with them.

這部電影很有趣，所以我跟他們留下來。

兩個單句 The audience was very excited. 與 I stayed with them. 藉由逗號（,）和對等連接詞 so 隔開而構成合句。

三、複句，也是由兩個或兩個以上的獨立子句所構成的，但是其中只有一個是主要子句，其他的都是附屬子句 (Dependent clause)，子句之間要用不對等連詞 (subordinate conjunction)，區分為

　㈠ 單純連詞：as, if, than, that, though, lest, when, since, while。

　㈡ 複合連詞：although, because, unless, whereas。

　㈢ 關聯連詞：as... as, as... so, so... as, so... that, whether... or。

（四）片語連詞：as soon as, as (or so) long as, as if, as though, in case, in order that, in that, for fear (that), the moment 等。

前述的答案有：

My father's <u>skin rashes</u> **when** he eats seafood and milk.
　　　　　　　S　　Vi

我父親吃海鮮和牛奶時，他的皮膚出疹子。

I usually <u>sneeze</u> and my respiratory <u>system</u> <u>becomes</u>
S　　　　Vi　　　　　　　　　　　　S　　Vi

<u>uncomfortable</u> **when** seasons change.
　　　SC

當四季變化的時候我經常打噴嚏，我的呼吸系統變得不舒服。

其他的例子：

Even though I <u>made a lot of money</u>, I lead a simple life.
即使我賺很多錢，我過著簡單的生活。

從屬子句"Even though I <u>made a lot of money</u>"後面跟著獨立子句"I lead a simple life."。

While <u>the cannon was firing</u>, the soldiers charged.
在大炮發射中，士兵們衝鋒。

從屬子句"**While** the cannon was firing"後面跟著獨立子句 "the soldiers charged."。

The soldiers charged **While** the cannon was firing. 我們也可以把從屬子句放在獨立子句之後。

Although she works the hardest in the class, she did the worst in the exams. 雖然她是班上最用功的，她卻考得很糟糕。

從屬子句"Although she's works the hardest in the class"放在 獨立子句"she did the worst in the exams."之前。

複句不一定是最長的句子，而單句也不一定是最短的句子，修飾語拉長了也可以是很長的句子，例如中華民國憲法序言就是一句單句，你可以試著找出主詞、動詞與受詞各在何處。

The National Assembly of the Republic of China, by virtue of the mandate received from the whole body of citizens, in accordance with the teachings bequeathed by Dr. Sun Yat-sen for founding of the Republic of China and in order to consolidate the sovereignty authority of the State, safeguard the rights of the people, ensure social tranquility, and promote the welfare of the people, does hereby establish this Constitution, to be promulgated throughout the country for faithful and perpetual observance by all.

　　中華民國國民大會受全體國民之付託，依據孫中山先生創立中華民國之遺教，為鞏固國權，保障民權，奠定社會安寧，增進人民福利，制定本憲法，頒行全國，永矢咸遵。

答案：

The National Assembly of the Republic of China establish this Constitution.

S	Vt	O

這一節我們接著介紹多益口說 7-9 題,這部分大致與 4-6 題的評分指標一樣,下表僅列特別針對 7-9 題的要求。

分數	回答情形
3	回答完整、符合問題和社交上的要求。在 7-9 題的情況下的資訊是準確的。
2	回答部分正確,但不能完整、適當、準確的回答問題。在 7-9 題的情況下的資訊不是充分準確的。
1	回應無法有效回答問題。無法成功的傳達相關資訊。
0	沒有回應或回應中不說英語,或回應與問題完全無關。

Questions 7–9: Respond to questions using information provided 聽錄音並複誦 🎧 **Mp3 013**

Directions: In this part of the test, you will answer three questions based on the information provided. You will have 30 seconds to read the information before the questions begin. For each question, begin responding immediately after you hear a beep. No additional preparation time is provided. You will have 15 seconds to respond to Questions 7 and 8, and 30 seconds to respond to Question 9.

問題 7-9：使用提供的資訊來回答問題：

說明：在此部分，你將依據提供的資訊回答三個問題。問題開始之前你有 30 秒閱讀資訊。聽到提示「嗶」音後開始回答每個問題。無額外的準備時間。你有 15 秒回答第 7 和 8 題，30 秒的時間回答第 9 題。

【Day 4】
Thursday

TOEIC Speaking
Question 7-11

聽錄音 Mp3 014

The Asia-Pacific Conference on Political Sciences

Date: Feb. 20th ~ Mar. 21th, 2014

Location: Hong Kong

The Asia-Pacific Conference on Political Science 2014 is one of the leading international conferences to present novel and fundamental advances in the fields of Political Science. It also serves to foster communication among researchers and practitioners working in a wide variety of scientific areas with a common interest in improving Political Science.

Keynote Speech:

"Influences of New Media And Technology On Cultural and Political Change"

Prof. John Tennyson, the author of *Influences of New Media And Technology On Cultural and Political Change*.

Book signing: 11: 00 A.M. Feb. 20th, Grand meeting Room.

Listen to the question:

This is Angela Norton. I am planning to attend the The Asia-Pacific Conference on Political Sciences, but I lost the original invitation, so I need some information.

Response time: 15 seconds

Question 7-11 亞太政治學會議

日期：2014 年 2 月 20 ～ 3 月 21 日

地點：香港

　　2014 年亞太區政治學會議，是提出新進展和基本政治科學領域領先的國際會議之一。它也有助於促進，在廣泛科學領域工作的研究人員和從業人員溝通。

主題演講：約翰·丁尼生教授主講

《新媒體和科技對文化和政治變遷的影響》一書作者。

簽書會：2 月 20 日上午 11:00 大會議廳。

聽問題：

　　我是安吉拉·諾頓。我打算去參加亞太政治學會議，但是遺失了原來的邀請函，所以我需要一些資訊。

回應時間：15 秒

TOEIC Speaking
Question 8-11

聽錄音 Mp3 015

Listen to the question:
I don't know who is Professor John Tennyson. Can you help me?

Response time: 15 seconds

Question 8-11

聽問題：我不知道誰是約翰‧丁尼生教授。你可以幫我嗎？

回應時間：15 秒

TOEIC Speaking
Question 9-11

聽錄音 Mp3 016

Listen to the question:
Besides the lecture from the main speaker, what else is going on?

Response time: 30seconds

Question 9-11

聽問題：

除了主講的講座，還有什麼活動？

回應時間：30 秒

Question 7-11 參考答案：　　　　　　　　聽錄音 🎧 Mp3 017

The conference will be held from February 20th to March 21th, 2014 in Hong Kong. Professor John Tennyson will deliver the keynote Speech.

會議將從 2 月 20 日至 2014 年 3 月 21 日於香港舉行。約翰‧丁尼生教授將發表專題演講。

Question 8-11 參考答案：　　　　　　　　聽錄音 🎧 Mp3 018

He is the author of *Influences of New Media And Technology On Cultural and Political Change*.

他是「新媒體和技術影響文化和政治的變化。」一書的作者。

Question 9-11 參考答案：　　　　　　　　聽錄音 🎧 Mp3 019

There will be a book signing at 11: 00 A.M., February 20th in the Grand meeting Room.

在 2 月 20 日上午 11:0，大會議廳將有一場簽書活動。

【Day 4】
Thursday

　　這是不同於英檢問答的題型，先提供一段會議議程或時間表，然後針對這些資料問三個問題，回答者必須按所提供的資料回答問題，評分也就如本節開始所列的表為標準。這種問答顯然不是單純的聽力理解問答而已，必須具備一定的閱讀能力才能有效應答。除了閱讀能力之外，我們所能加強自己回答正確能力的方法，還是前幾節所做的，把自己回答的內容寫下來，然後檢查自己文句上的文法、用字等等問題。

　　前兩節我們檢查的重點是句型與句構，這一節我們就題目多涉及時間問題，所以也檢討一下時態的問題。

　　先就題目中的時態來探討：

　　不論我們現在的時間是在 2014 年之前或後，這是一則會議通知，自然是未來發生的事情。所以用現在簡單式"is"敘述「2014 年政治學亞太區會議，是提出新進展和基本政治科學領域領先的國際會議之一。」

　　既然是即將要進行的會議，也就用現在簡單式的"helps"來敘述「它也有助於促進研究人員和從業人員，在廣泛科學領域工作與提高政治學的共同興趣之間的溝通。」

　　問題 7「我打算去參加亞太政治學會議，但是遺失了原來的邀請信，所以我需要一些資訊。」「打算」是有計畫、準備要「做」的事，所以用"am planning to..."。而「遺失」了邀請函是已經發生的事情，所以要用過去簡單式"lost"。而回答會議資訊是敘述一件未來會「發生」的事，所以用"will"表達。

問題 8 以及答案都是敘述確認不變的事實，不知道對方是誰以及回答對方是誰，所以用現在簡單式"I don't know..." "He is..."表達。

問題 9 對於簽書會用"is going on"表示某事「一定會發生」的一個片語，換一種說法也可以問"what other events will there be?"所以回答還是用"will"表達。除了現在、現在進行與未來式，我們也可看看其他時態對舉行會議的說法：

There will be another conference going on during the session of this one.

這一屆會議期間將會將會有另一次會議進行。（未來進行式）

There has been a conference.

現在已經有一場會議了。（現在完成式）

The conference has been going off for 3 days.

會議進行 3 天了。（現在完成進行式）

There was a conference.

曾經有過一次會議。（過去簡單式）

Other small group discussions in the conference were going on when the professor made his speech.

教授發表演說當時，其他小組討論也同時進行。（過去完成進行式）

The conference had started before the professor made speech.

教授演講之前會議已經開始了。（過去完成式）

再做一回全民英檢口說測驗的 II. 回答問題，然後再以前三節所練習的五大句型、三大句構和時態三個文法重點來檢查。

這個部分共有 10 題。題目已事先錄音，每題經由耳機播出二次，不印在試題冊上。第 1 至 5 題，每題回答時間 15 秒；第 6 至 10 題，每題回答時間 30 秒。每題播出後，請立即回答。回答時，不一定要用完整的句子，但請在作答時間內儘量的表達。

現在請聽錄音並按每題播出後 15 秒與 30 秒的時限作答，作答後最好把自己的答案寫下來，一來可以順便練習寫作，二來可以參考答案對照，看看有無用字、結構與文法上的錯誤。

請聽錄音 🎧 Mp3 020

Question 1: Describe your father.

（15 秒）

Question 2: Are you an organized person? Why or why not?

（15 秒）

Question 3: You're watching a movie in a theater. Suddenly, the fire alarm goes off. What will you do next?

（15 秒）

Question 4: Why are there more and more problems of food security?

（15 秒）

Question 5: What are two things we should pay attention to when we drive? Why?

（**15 秒**）

Question 6: Do you go hiking a lot? If so, tell me about your experience. If not, tell me something you know about hiking.

（**30 秒**）

Question 7: Tell me one of your hobbies? Why do you like it?

（**30 秒**）

Question 8: What kinds of foods should you eat to be healthy? Why?

（**30 秒**）

Question 9: Why is it important to reduce energy use?

（**30 秒**）

Question 10: Describe your favorite free time activity. How was it last time?

（**30 秒**）

【Day 5】
Friday

參考答案

每題請聽錄音並複誦 🎧 Mp3 021

Question 1

My father is an English teacher. He is a little strict, but good father. He is very patient with us just as he is with his students. He gave us the goals of life with simple, but firm instructions.

我的父親是一名英語老師。他有點嚴格，但是一個好的父親。他對我們正如對他的學生一樣很有耐心。他以簡單而堅定的指導引領我們人生目標。

🎧 Mp3 022

My father is a military man. He is unbending in setbacks and humble and gentle when he gets ahead. He always tells us that knowing ourselves is the foundation of knowledge.

我的父親是一名軍人。他在挫折中不屈不撓，在順境中卻保持謙遜。他總是告訴我們，了解自我是知識的基礎。

每題請聽錄音並複誦 🎧 Mp3 023

Question 2

Yes, I'm an organized person. I keep my room tidy, my bed clean, and never forget doing the laundry. I have never been late for school, and I turn in my assignments on time.

是的，我是有條理的人。我總是保持房間整齊，床舖乾淨，從不耽誤衣物洗滌。而且在此基礎上，我從不上班遲到，我準時完成我的作業。

Mp3 024

No, I'm not an organized person. My room is always messy with dirty underwear, smelly socks, and scattered books. What's worse, I can't catch up with schedules, and my works are often overdue.

不，我不是有條理的人。我的房間總是雜亂，髒內衣、臭襪子和書四處散亂。更糟的是，我老趕不上進度，我的工作經常超過時限。

每題請聽錄音並複誦 Mp3 025

Question 3

Actually, I don't know what to do then. Since the panic crowd may be in my way, I will rush the faster the better. If the smoke gets dense, I guess all I could do is to stay low and crawl to the nearest exit.

實際上我還沒有什麼想法。由於人群恐慌的人群可能擋住我的路，我會衝得越快越好。如果煙霧濃密，我能做的就是盡量蹲低，爬到最近的出口。

Mp3 026

If the alarm goes off, I will inform the people around me there is a fire. Next, I will tell people to follow the emergency instruction, and then assist individuals with disabilities and others if it is safe to do so.

如果警報響起的時候，我會通知我周圍的人有火災。接下來，我將告訴人們要遵守一切緊急指令，然後在安全情況下協助殘疾人。

【Day 5】Friday

每題請聽錄音並複誦 Mp3 027

Question 4

I think government agencies fail to protect their citizens from consuming tainted oil. Food companies are the ones to be blamed. After all, they buy that oil, knowing that the source is from the recycled waste oil. What's worse, they sold it to loyal customers. maintain foremost control in protecting our food supply. That's why the food company was able to buy recycled waste oil and mix it with lard oil to resell to customers.

　　我認為政府機關未能在圓頭把好關。食品公司該被譴責。畢竟，他們知情來源是回收的廢油，卻買了。更糟的是，他們還是賣給了他們的忠實客戶，主張最先掌控維護我們食物供給。這就是為什麼食品公司能夠回收廢油，然後混豬油以轉賣給客戶。

🎧 Mp3 028

I think the tainted oil is the main cause of our food safety problems. Tons of popular products, including seasonal mooncakes, pineapple cakes, breads, instant noodles, steamed buns, and dumplings have been contaminated.

　　我覺得污染油是我國食品安全問題的主要原因。成噸的常用食品，包括節慶月餅、鳳梨酥、麵包、速食麵、饅頭和餃子等等都已經被污染。

每題請聽錄音並複誦 Mp3 029

Question 5

I think talking and texting are the two main driver distractions on the driver's list. Using a cellphone while driving is illegal, let alone texting messages.

我認為聊天和發短信是使駕駛分心的兩件危險事。我們不能一手握方向盤另一手拿著手機，更別說還同時發簡訊。

🎧 Mp3 030

I think daydreaming while driving is also very dangerous, and it's one of the most serious problems on the driving list. The problem will be aggravated by fatigue and a wandering mind. We should sleep well before driving and focus on the road right in front of us.

我認為在方向盤後面做白日夢是駕駛最嚴重的問題。問題在疲勞和心不在焉。我們應該在開車前睡好覺並專注於我們眼前的道路上。

【Day 5】
Friday

每題請聽錄音並複誦 🎧 Mp3 031

Question no. 6

I like hiking. It's a healthy way to spend wonderful time with friends. Hiking is a good way to get some exercise. It's a mixture of excellent aerobic activities and life enjoyment. The experience of hiking is unimaginable. It has created an unforgettable memory in your life. Hiking doesn't necessarily have to take high risk and difficult challenge. Hiking can be done in any wooded area or even a local public park.

我喜歡徒步旅行。它是和朋友一起度過美好時光的健康方式。徒步旅行是種得到鍛鍊及優質有氧活動很好途徑。徒步旅行的經驗會留給你生命中難忘的回憶。徒步旅行並不一定要採取高風險和困難的挑戰，也可以在任何樹木繁茂的區域或甚至當地的公園進行。

🎧 Mp3 032

Although I'm not familiar with hiking, I know gear is the necessity. Hiking can be a pleasant activity, if everyone is outfitted in the appropriate gear. For example, comfortable sneakers or hiking boots, a backpack big enough, light enough to carry all of the snacks and other things you will need on the trail. Make sure that you have a good camera so that you can record memories along the way.

雖然我不熟悉徒步旅行，我知道裝備是必需品。如果每個人都配備了妥善的裝備，徒步旅行是可以令人愉快的活動。例如，舒適的運動鞋或者徒步旅行靴，夠大也夠輕的背包，可攜帶所有的小吃和其他路上需要的東西。請確保您有一台好相機，以便記錄沿途的回憶。

每題請聽錄音並複誦 🎧 Mp3 033

Question 7

Writing software is my hobby. During my years at college, I helped create a website to solve all homework problems. Even today, some of my classmates are my big fans of the website. Since then the software has now been a part of people's life.

我喜歡以編寫軟體作為一種愛好。在大學期間，我協助創建了一個為解決所有作業的問題的網站。即使在今天，我的一些同學都是我網站上的大粉絲。它現在已經是人們的生活的一部分。

 Mp3 034

My hobbies are mostly restricted to outdoor activities. Among all hobbies, fishing is my favorite. I like to have fishing trips with friends. I started fishing at the age of 13, and now I run a fishing club with hundreds of members. The hobby not only gives me a great pleasure, but a good career life. However, I am also an environmentalist; I do go fishing for fun, but will never damage the ecological balance.

我的愛好多半是戶外活動。所有愛好中釣魚是我最喜愛的。我喜歡與朋友一起釣魚。我十三歲開始釣魚，現在我經營一個有數百名成員的釣魚俱樂部。這個愛好不僅給我很大的樂趣，也成為很好的職業。然而，我也是一個環保主義者；我釣魚，但從來沒有破壞任何生態平衡。

【Day 5】Friday

每題請聽錄音並複誦 Mp3 035

Question 8

Acid Fruits, such as lemons, oranges, grapefruits, peaches, limes, tangerines, grapes, tomatoes, pineapples, apples, are the most detoxifying ingredients. Some people may have problems with these fruits because of their acid content. The acid though is a healthy and organic nutritional element; for instance, ascorbic acid is vitamin C, found especially in citrus fruits and vegetables.

酸的水果，如檸檬、柳丁、葡萄柚、桃子、酸橙、柑橘、葡萄、番茄、鳳梨、蘋果等等，是最具解毒和優良的食物。有些人可能受不了這些水果的酸度，這種酸卻是一個健康和有機的營養要素，例如，抗壞血酸是維生素 C，尤其在柑桔類水果和蔬菜中含量最高。

🎧 Mp3 036

Rye bread and flaxseed bread are the healthiest types of bread that you can eat daily without worrying about calories. They are fantastic bread for weight loss and it's an excellent source of mineral ingredients. Flaxseed bread also contains essential fatty acids and dietary fiber that will help boost your health and get your dreamed body shape. Rye bread is absolutely wheat-free, and it can help relieve discomfort and bloating.

黑麥麵包和亞麻籽麵包是最健康的兩種麵包，你可以每天吃而不用擔心卡路里含量。他們是減肥的神奇麵包，有極好礦物成分。亞麻籽麵包還含精華的脂肪酸和膳食纖維，有助於提昇你的健康，讓你有個夢想的體態。黑麥麵包絕對不含小麥，它可以減輕煩悶和腹脹。

每題請聽錄音並複誦 🎧 Mp3 037

Question 9

While we need Energy to power our cars, cook our food, light up our homes, and so much more, many of us become wasteful and actually use much more than we actually need. This excess can cause unnecessary, avoidable pollution. Pollution harms the air quality that we inhale outside. It also negatively impacts wildlife, such as plants, trees, and animals.

即使我們需要消耗能量，以提供我們的汽車動力、做飯、照明、還有很多需求，很多人還是浪費，而且實際上消耗遠多過我們真正需要的能源。這些過多消耗導致不必要的、能避免的污染。污染損害我們戶外所吸入的空氣品質。它也對野生動物如植物、產生了不利的影響。

Mp3 038

Energy savings can help us from a financial standpoint. Since energy is in higher and higher demand, prices continue to rise, costing householders a fortune. When you reduce your energy use, you are able to cut down on your energy bills, so that more money can be saved from your pocket! Our hard-earned money shouldn't be wasted on energy in places of things we truly want.

節約能源可以從財務方面對我們助益。由於能源是越來越高的需求，價格持續上漲，住家負擔沈重。當你減少能源使用時，可以減少你的電費，所以從你的口袋裡省下來更多的錢！我們不應該把辛苦賺來的錢浪費在電費上，而該用在我們真正想要的東西上。

【Day 5】Friday

每題請聽錄音並複誦 Mp3 039

Question 10

My favorite free time activity is hiking. Last time, I hiked Ali Mountain, which is worldwide famous for its "five rare sites" including the Sunrise, the Ali Mountain Forest Railway, the famous Alishan Sacred Tree, the Grand Sea of Clouds, and the Flamboyant Cherry Blossom. I would never known its wonderful beauty before paying a visit there.

我最喜歡的空閒時間的活動是徒步旅行。上次去了阿里山健行，它有全球著名的日出、森林鐵路、神木、壯觀的雲海和豔麗盛開的櫻花等「五個罕見的景點」。未去過那裡之前，我從不知道它的神奇美景。

🎧 Mp3 040

My favorite free time activity is fishing. Last time, I went fishing at Sun Moon Lake. The weather was beautiful that day. I consulted with a local guide to get the actual sunrise and sunset plus moon rise and moon set timetable. My fishing trip was successful and I caught a full bag of Tilapia. They are fun to catch.

釣魚我最喜歡的空閒時間的活動。上次我去了日月潭釣魚。那天天氣很好。我諮詢了一個當地的導遊，來說明該挑選什麼時候接觸水面，每天日出和日落、以及月升和月落時間。我的釣魚之旅很成功，我釣了滿滿一袋子的福壽魚。抓牠們很有趣。

讀完了參考答案之後，接下來就是針對這些題目的答案做句型、句構、以及時態的檢查。前幾節我們已經針對基本的句子分析過了，這一節我們只選擇較複雜的句子分析就可以了。是將下一段選文畫底線的地方標註句型詞類，並在每句的句尾括弧處寫下句構類型。

Energy savings can help us from a financial standpoint. (   ) Since energy is in a higher and higher demand, prices continue to rise, costing householders a fortune. (   )

When you reduce your energy use, <u>you</u> <u>are</u> <u>able</u> to cut down on your energy bills, so <u>there</u> <u>is</u> more <u>money</u> saved from your pocket!（　　　）Our hard earned <u>money</u> shouldn't <u>be</u> <u>wasted</u> on energy in places of things we truly want.（　　　）

試對下一段選文化底線的動詞，解釋其時態的用法：

My favorite free time activity **is** hiking. Last time, I **hiked** Ali Mountain, which **is** worldwide famous for its "five rare sites" including the Sunrise, the Ali Mountain Forest Railway, the famous Alishan Sacred Tree, the Grand Sea of Clouds, and the Flamboyant Cherry Blossom. I would never know its wonderful beauty before I paying a visit there.

參考答案：

句型句構：

Energy <u>savings</u> can <u>help</u> <u>us</u> from a financial standpoint.
　　　　 S 　　　　 Vt O

（單句）Since energy is in higher and higher demand, <u>prices</u>
　　　　　　　　　　　　　　　　　　　　　　　　　　　　　 S

<u>continue</u> to <u>rise</u>, costing householders a fortune.（複句）When
　Vt　　　　 O

you reduce your energy use, <u>you</u> <u>are</u> <u>able</u> to cut down on your
　　　　　　　　　　　　　　　 S

energy bills, so <u>there</u> more <u>money</u> can be saved from your
　　　　　　　　　 S　　　　 SC

pocket!（合句 ❶）Our hard earned <u>money</u> shouldn't <u>be</u> <u>wasted</u>

                                   S   Vi SC

on energy in places of things we truly want.（複句）

動詞時態：

My favorite free time activity **is** hiking. Last time,

                                "is"是現在簡單式表習慣的用法。

I **hiked** Ali Mountain, which **is** worldwide famous for its "five

  "hiked"是過去簡單式表做過的事。   "is"是現在簡單式表事實。

rare sites" including the Sunrise, the Ali Mountain Forest Railway,

the famous Alishan Sacred Tree, the Grand Sea of Clouds, and the

Flamboyant Cherry Blossom. I would never know its wonderful

beauty before I paying a visit there.

---

❶ 有些文法書將此類結構稱為「合複句」(compound complex sentence) 或「混合句」，其實這種句子還是以對等連詞連接的兩個對等觀念。

WEEK2

簡短對話篇

WEEK 2 簡短對話篇

以下是全民英檢與多益聽力測驗的模擬題，稍早之前，我們已經做了口說延伸的練習，接下來我們再把範圍擴張到簡短對話方向，先練習聽力作答後，再分析整段對話的主旨大意與重要細節，培養下一步自己進行較長篇幅的對話能力。我們先用多益的聽力對話題練習 12 題，然後分析這些題型分別要求聽者理解內容的是大意還是細節。

請聽錄音 Mp3 041

Part 3

Directions: In this section of the test, you will hear a number of conversations between two people. You will be asked to answer three questions about what is said in each conversation. You must select the best response to each question and mark the letter (A) ,(B), (C), or (D) on your answer sheet. Each conversation will be spoken only one time and will not be printed in your test book.

Question 1 and 2 refer to the following conversation

1. What is true about the report?
   (A) The inmates were caught stealing guns.
   (B) The floor of the prison has a tunnel under it.
   (C) It happened last month.
   (D) The inmates climbed up the roof and ran away.

2. What will the jail probably do next?
   (A) Move to a new place
   (B) Look for the inmates
   (C) Look for the tunnel
   (D) Put them in the report

Question 3 to 5 refer to the following conversation

Mp3 042

3. What will happen tomorrow morning?

   (A) Carter will call Mr. James.

   (B) Carter will see Mr. James.

   (C) Carter will take a subway.

   (D) Carter will buy a mobile phone.

4. When might be the time that they see each other?

   (A) 10 o'clock

   (B) 11 o'clock

   (C) 12 o'clock

   (D) 1 o'clock

5. What will Mr. James do next?

   (A) He will answer Carter's question.

   (B) He will tell Carter what to buy.

   (C) He will pick him up in Central Park.

   (D) He will meet him in 5th Avenue.

Question 6 to 8 refer to the following conversation

 Mp3 043

6. Why did the woman sell the car?

   (A) She wanted a smaller vehicle.

   (B) She wanted a budget one.

   (C) She wanted a new one.

   (D) She wanted a four-wheel drive one.

7. Where does this conversation take place?

   (A) In a gas station

   (B) In the country

   (C) In the woman's place

   (D) In a car dealership

8. What will happen next?

   (A) They will leave the town.

   (B) They will drive out of the country.

   (C) The man will see a car.

   (D) The man will sell a car.

Question 9 to 10 refer to the following conversation

 Mp3 044

9. What happened to the man last night?

    (A) Someone took his job.

    (B) He was checked by the company.

    (C) He had good luck.

    (D) He called his wife for help.

10. What is the man probably "NOT" going to do next?

    (A) Get a better place

    (B) Change the office

    (C) Get a new job

    (D) Beg his former boss

Question 11 to 12 refer to the following conversation

 Mp3 045

11. What will happen if Denis goes on the trip?

    (A) She will visit Japan.

    (B) She will go alone.

    (C) She will stay in a couch.

    (D) She will go for less than two weeks.

12. Why didn't Denis's father just say "Yes"?

    (A) He wanted to go with Denis.

    (B) His wife hasn't say "Yes" yet.

    (C) He probably thinks Denis is too young.

    (D) He doesn't know Yvonne and Sonia.

答案：

1. B 2.B 3.C 4.C 5.A 6.B 7.C 8.D 9.C 10.D 11. D 12.B

做完「簡短對話」聽力練習後，我們要注意的，除了聽力得分高低之外，還要延伸這項聽力測驗的「簡短對話」內容分析，以便自己也能做簡短對話的練習。

多益的簡短對話題型大致以 W 開頭的問句最普遍，問理由、時間、地點或特定細節以及推論等等如下：

1. Why did the man invite Mr. James?
2. What is the woman talking about?
3. When is the brief going to take place?
4. How many employees are working in the company?
5. Who is going to take part in the meeting?
6. What does the director imply about the new rules?

第一、二類題目屬於主旨大意的問題，第三至五題屬於細節題，第六題屬於推論題。下面我們就以剛才練習的題目讓大家辨識看看各種題目屬於哪一類。

1. What is true about the report?
2. What will the jail probably do next?
3. What will happen tomorrow morning?
4. When might be the time when they see each other?
5. What will Mr. James do next?
6. Why did the woman sell the car?
7. Where does this conversation take place?

8. What will happen next?

9. What happened to the man last night?

10. What is the man probably "NOT" going to do next?

11. What will happen if Denis goes on the trip?

12. Why didn't Denis's father just say "Yes"?

　　第 6、9、12 屬於主旨大意題。第 1、4、7、8 屬於細節題。第 2、3、5、10、11 屬於推論（預測）題。

　　主旨題的範圍必須能完整的涵蓋整個內容，以第三題為例，若單回答明天會發生甚麼事，我們一般的判斷是四個答案好像都對，但是對話內容的主旨是買手機，因此就只能選 D 答案。其他的答案雖然都對，卻都只是細節。這也是多益測驗的一個特色，要求的答案不只是正確 (correct) 還要是最好的 (best) 答案。英檢中級以上則要求「最適合」的答案。

(A) Carter will call Mr. James.（細節）

(B) Carter will see Mr. James.（細節）

(C) Carter will take a subway.（細節）

(D) Carter will buy a mobile phone.（主旨）

　　第三類的推論（預測）題，是猜測字句所暗示的意義，如 What does the man mean? 或預測將發生的事，如第 10.What is the man probably "NOT" going to do next? 以及第 11. What will happen if Denis goes on the trip?

不過，所謂預測、推論也是依據內容很明確的證據得到的，如第 11 題問那人可能不會做的是甚麼事，現在他有了更好的新差事，自然最不可能的就是再回去求舊東家，因為眼前就是這個舊東家不要他的。

有了這三種題型的歸類，我們就可以在自己編一段對話時，注意先掌握主旨然後來引導細節與推論，這樣一篇對話就不會偏離主題或散亂無章了。例如第一篇對話（第 1、2 題）的主旨是逃犯如何逃出監獄 (How did the inmates get out?) 如果我們想繼續延伸話題就應該繼續討論地道是怎麼挖的，而偷槍就不是談話主軸了。下面就以原對話為基礎，大家試試延伸話題：

第 2 題 What will the inmates probably do next? 正好就是可延伸的主題。

1-2

Man: Anything important in that report?
在那篇報導中有什麼重要事呢？

Woman: Well, three inmates fled last night. They also stole 3 guns.
有吧，昨晚三名囚犯逃獄了。他們還偷走了三把槍。

Man: How did the inmates get out?
囚犯是如何逃出來的？

Woman:They made a tunnel under the floor and crawled out of the prison. But how they stole the guns is not known. Maybe they stole them at some other time.

他們在地板下挖一條地道，爬出了監獄。但不是知道他們如何偷到槍的。也許是在其他時間偷走的。

延伸部分

請聽音檔 🎧 Mp3 046

Now listen to the following conversation 問題 2 即可為話頭

Man: What do you think the inmates will probably do next?

你認為囚犯下一步可能會做什麼？

Woman: Of course, they should find the inmates as soon as possible!

當然要儘快找到犯人！

Man: What if they can't find them? These fugitives are walking time bombs with deadly weapons.

如果他們找不到他們呢？這些逃犯是身懷致命武器的不定時炸彈。

Woman: I guess the law enforcement agencies are going to have a hard time.

我想執法機關的日子該不好過了吧！

下面就試試第二篇的延伸對話：

3-5

Man 1: Hello, Mr. James. My name's Tony. I'd like to buy a mobile phone, but I know nothing about them. Can you help?

你好，詹姆士先生。我的名字叫托尼。我想要買一部手機，但我對它們一無所知。你能說明嗎？

Man 2: It'd be better if you could come and see me and we'll find the right mobile phone for you.

最好是你能來找我，我們會為您找到合用的行動電話。

Man 1: Oh! Great! I'll come in tomorrow. I'll take the subway at 10 o'clock. I think I have to change in Center Park, but it is a short wait and I will arrive in 5th Avenue at 11 o'clock. Can you tell me how far it is from the station to your company?

哦！很好！我明天會來。我會在上午 10 點乘坐地鐵。我想我要中央公園轉車，但不會等太久，我在 11 點以前可以到達第五大道。你能告訴我從車站到貴公司有多遠嗎？

（延伸對話）

4. When might be the time when they see each other? 正好可以是話題的開始

請聽音檔 🎧 Mp3 047

Now listen to the following conversation

Man 1: Hello, Mr. James. It's Tony and I have arrived at 5th Avenue right now at 11 o'clock but I really got lost around the block here. Could you tell me how to find your shop?

你好，詹姆士先生。我是托尼，現在是上午 11 點，我到了第五大道車站，但我在這一帶真的迷路了。你能告訴我怎樣才能找到你的店嗎？

Man 2: Try to find the cross road sign for East 36th Street and 5th Avenue. There is a tall building with the Stars and Stripes on the pillars. Just wait there at the corner, and I'll personally pick you up.

試著找東 36 街和第五大道的十字路標誌。那裡有一座高樓，柱子上掛著美國國旗。就在轉角那兒等著，我親自去接你。

Man 1: Thanks a lot!

多謝！

依照上兩段的延伸方式，大家再試試其餘的三段對話。

6-8

Man: This was a nice car. I thought you had a great time driving.

這曾是一輛好車。我認為你駕駛得很愉快。

Woman: I used to, but I sold it. It was a four-wheel drive vehicle, consuming too much fuel for me. Besides, I have already had a smaller car. It's a more economical one.

我曾經是，但我賣了它。這是四輪驅動車，對我來說太耗油。何況，我有一輛小車。它是一輛比較省錢的車。

Man: That sounds great. Can I see it sometime?

聽起來很棒。有空時我能看一下嗎？

Woman: Of course. It's in the garage if you like to see it now.

當然可以。如果你想看，就在車庫裡。

9-10

Man: I had a wonderful night yesterday. While I was worrying about losing my job, the other company called me to offer a better place. When I checked my account, I found a generous payment in advance!

昨天是個美妙的夜晚。我正在擔心失去工作的時候，另一家公司來電話通知給我一個更好的職位。當我查看我的帳戶時，發現他們已經慷慨的預付了薪水！

Woman: Did you call your wife right away?

你馬上就告訴你的妻子了嗎？

Man: Yes, and she said I would never let her down.

是的她說：我從不會讓她失望。

Woman: Well, I bet you are!

是吧，我敢打賭你是！

6-8 參考答案

8. What will happen next? 正好是話頭

請聽音檔 🎧 Mp3 048

Now listen to the following conversation

Man: This car is brand new. Why do you want to sell it too?
這輛車是全新的。為什麼你也要賣？

Woman: Well, I'm moving to another country. Everything you see around is about to be auctioned later.
是這樣，我要搬去其他國家。你所看到的一切都是稍後要拍賣的。

Man: Why didn't you say so? You could have put this car together with others in an ad of auction.
你為什麼不早說？你大可以把這輛車與其他東西一起放進一則拍賣廣告中。

Woman: Because I know you are a car lover. The car deserves a better owner.
因為我知道你是一個汽車愛好者。這輛車值得更好的擁有者。

請聽音檔 Mp3 049

Now listen to the following conversation

9-10

10. What is the man probably "NOT" going to do next? 正好可為
話頭）

Man: I can't wait to see the look of my boss when I tell him I'm going to leave.

當我告訴老闆要離開的時候，我迫不及待想看他的表情。

Woman: I don't think that will make him surprised. After all, you are to leave whether you quit or not.

我不認為那會讓他感到驚訝。畢竟，你辭不辭職都是要離開的。

Now listen to the following conversation

11-12

Woman: Dad, I want to take part in the marathon in China with Yvonne and Sonia.

爸爸，我想和伊馮娜和索尼婭參加中國馬拉松賽。

Man: I'm not sure, Denis. Who is coaching you?

我不確定可否答應，丹妮絲。誰是你的教練？

Woman: Mr. Louis, you know him. We've practiced for months and we are all in good shape. Everything for the race is ready. We would go for ten days to two weeks.

是陸義士先生，你認識他的。我們已經練習了幾個月，我們都處於良好狀態。一切為比賽的準備都就緒。我們要去十天到兩個禮拜。

Man: I'll talk to your mother this evening. But I'm not making any promises.

今天晚上我會跟你的母親談。但我不會做出任何承諾。

11-12 參考答案

請聽音檔 🎧 **Mp3 050**

12. Why didn't Denis's father just say "Yes"? 即可為話頭。

Woman: Why don't you just say "Yes," Dad? It's your idea asking me to play more sports, and Mom also said she would wholeheartedly endorse it.
爸爸你為什麼就是不說好？是你的主意要求我去做更多運動，媽媽也說她會全心全意地贊同。

Man: Yes, that's what I said, but I didn't expect that China is your concern. It's such a long journey of some where you have never been before, and how do I know that you will be taken care of as it is due?
沒錯，是我所說的，但我沒想到你去的是中國。它是一趟你沒去過如此漫長的旅程，和我怎麼知道你能否受到應有的照顧？

Woman: Daddy, I'm a big girl now. I know what I'm doing!
爸爸，我現在已經是一個大女孩了。我知道自己在做什麼！

Man: Just let me ask your mother's opinion, and see if she is still agree to it now.
讓我問你媽媽的意見，看看她現在是否還同意。

DAY ② TUESDAY

下面我們練習一段英檢的簡短對話聽力測驗。先練習聽力作答後，再分析整段對話的主旨大意與重要細節，進一步自己進行較長篇幅的對話。

第三部份：簡短對話

本部份共 15 題，每題請聽錄音機播出一段對話及一個相關的問題後，從試題冊上 A、B、C、D 四個備選答案中找出一個最適合的回答。每段對話及問題只播出一遍。

請聽音檔 Mp3 051

Directions: In this section of the test, you will hear a number of conversations between two people. You will be asked to answer three questions about what is said in each conversation. You must select the best response to each question and mark the letter (A) ,(B), (C), or (D) on your answer sheet. Each conversation will be spoken only one time and will not be printed in your test book.

31. A. To give a present.

    B. To make a request.

    C. To see him off.

    D. To bring something abroad.

32. A. A teacher.

    B. A tattoo artist.

    C. A policeman.

    D. A newsreader.

33. A. In a grocery store.

    B. In a farm.

    C. In a book store.

    D. In a restaurant.

34. A. A commercial site.

    B. A place to go shopping.

    C. A sale in the station.

    D. A sale's manner.

35. A. From a TV program.

    B. From an art gallery.

    C. From a song.

    D. From an art magazine.

36. A. He missed the train again.

    B. He got lost on the way.

    C. He forgot the meeting.

    D. He had a problem with his car.

37. A. The bags are not packed.

    B. She can't stay overnight.

    C. They ran out of money.

    D. He won't pay with check.

38. A. He can take bus.

    B. He has to take a rapid transit train first.

    C. He has to transfer buses.

    D. He can get off at 101 station.

39. A. She has called the police about the accident.

    B. She doesn't know what to do.

    C. She is frightened seeing police.

    D. She is trying to run away.

40. A. Their baggage isn't ready yet.

    B The man is packing up.

    C. He ordered the tickets.

    D. She forgot when to arrive.

41. A. She'll be late for the party today.

    B. She'll do the make-up for Cindy.

    C. She wants to cancel their party date.

    D. She wants Cindy to prepare for the role play at the party.

42. A. The entertainment industry.

    B. The project of New York.

    C. The tour in New York.

    D. The hangouts in New York.

43. A. His plan on journalism is very interesting.

    B. He was a paper boy.

    C. He seems to lack ambition.

    D. He has the potential to be a journalist.

44. A. Go to the book store.

    B. Wait for the returning people.

    C. Arrange some book shelves.

    D. Go for a date later.

45. A. It's too far away from the woman's office.

    B. It's too small.

    C. It's too tricky.

    D. It's too noisy downtown.

【Day 2】Tuesday

答案：

31. B　32. A　33. D　34. B　35. A　36. D　37. C　38. B
39. B　40. A　41. D　42. A　43. D　44. C　45. C

31. Why did the woman talk to the man?

32. Who is the man?

33. Where did this conversation take place?

34. What are the speakers talking about?

35. Where did the woman learn about "Vincent"?

36. Why is Steven late?

37. Why do they have to check out?

38. According to the woman, how can the man get to the Taipei 101?

39. What does Anny mean?

40. What does the man mean?

41. What message did Maggi leave?

42. What is the woman ready to study?

43. What do the two speakers think about John?

44. What will Mendy and Jason probably do next?

45. What does the woman think about the job?

　　如上一節我們學過的，主旨題的範圍必須能完整的涵蓋整個內容，如地 31、34、36、37、39、43，相對來說第 32、33、35、38、41、42、45 就是細節問題了。推論（預測）題，是猜測字句所暗示的意義，如第 44。全民英檢的簡短對話題是一段對話一題，所以那個問題也是很關鍵的話頭，我們練習延伸這些對話時，就可以用問題來延伸，但是由於這些問題未必是對話的主旨，我們還是要注意掌握這段對話的主軸，以免言不及義。如第 32 問的是說話的男人是誰，但主旨是爭論有無作弊的行為，而且說話的女人當然知道男人是老師，繼續的話題絕不可能問這男人是誰。下面我們就繼續練習延伸對話，這一回聽力測驗有 15 題，我們就分兩節練習，這一節先練習四段對話。

31. W：Tom, are you going abroad tomorrow?

　　　湯姆，你明天要出國嗎？

　　M：Yes, why?

　　　是，有事嗎？

　　W：Could you bring me a bottle of perfume from the duty free store when you come back? I need one of Chanel.

　　　當你回來的時候，能幫我從免稅商店帶一瓶香奈兒香水嗎？

　　M：Sure, no problem.

　　　當然，沒問題。

32. M：Can I see your paper, please?
　　我能看看你的試卷嗎？

　　W：I wasn't cheating, was I?
　　我沒作弊，對吧？

　　M：That's what I'm trying to find out.
　　那是我正要查明的。

　　W：I do all the answers by myself. Look, here they are.
　　所有的答案都是我自己做的。你看，都在這裡。

　　M：Then, you should put them only on your sheet, not on your legs.
　　那你應該把它們寫在考卷上，而不是雙腿上。

　　W：They are just my tattoos. Please, don't take my paper away, sir.
　　那只是我的紋身。請不要把我的考卷收走，老師。

　　M：Sorry.
　　抱歉。

（延伸參考答案）

31. W: Tom, you are back! Good to see you again! How is your trip?

湯姆，你回來了！很高興再次見到你！這趟出差如何？

M: Well, it is basically alright. Oh! This is your perfume, the Chanel Number 5.

還好，過得去。哦！這是你的香水，香奈兒 5 號。

W: Wow! Thank you, and how much do I owe you?

哇！謝謝你，我該給你多少錢？

M: Well, just take it as a gift. After all, I awed you a lot as my deputy when I was away.

好了，就算一份禮物。畢竟，我不在辦公室的時候多虧你代理我的很多業務。

W: How sweet of you, but it's still too much for me.

你真窩心，但對我來說，這禮還是太重了。

M: Don't mention it anymore if you seriously take me as a friend.

如果你認真地把我當成朋友就別再提了。

32. W: Sir, you haven't even looked close to my legs! How can you just make the arbitrary assertion?

老師，你根本沒仔細看我的腿！你如何能武斷地確認？

M: I don't think it's appropriate to look at a lady's legs in public, but I did see you checking your legs out with your answers. If you insist on your innocence, we can turn to the dean's office and have another lady make sure what those are on your legs.

我認為不適宜在公眾面前看一位女士的腿，但確實看到你作答時一直查看你的腿。如果你堅持你的清白，我們可以到院長辦公室並請另一位女士來確認你腿上的是甚麼。

33. W: Can I help you?

有甚麼我可以服務的嗎？

M: Yes, I'd like two bags of flour, a dozen eggs, and a bottle of milk.

是的，我想要兩袋麵粉，一打雞蛋和一瓶牛奶。

W: Two bags of flour, a dozen eggs, and a bottle of milk. Low fat or full cream?

兩袋麵粉，一打雞蛋和一瓶牛奶。低脂或全脂的？

M: Low fat, please.

低脂的，麻煩你

W： And by credit card or in cash?
刷卡，還是付現？

M： Credit card. Here you are.
信用卡。給你。

W： O.K. That's $155. Have a nice day.
好了！這樣是 155 美元。祝您有美好的一天。

34. M： Judy, I think you might be excited by this commercial. Cosmetics are on sale at Sincere.
茱蒂，我想你可能會對這個廣告興奮。先施百貨開始化妝品特賣會。

W： Sincere? Oh, is that near the MRT station at First Avenue?
先施百貨嗎？噢，就是在第一大道地鐵站附近那一家嗎？

M： Yes, that's the one. Here's the website.
就是那個。這裡是網站。

W： Thanks. I'll be ready to purchase a lot.
謝謝你。我會準備買很多的。

（延伸參考答案）

33. M： Oh! By the way, I heard you are going to have a big sale recently.

哦！順便問一句，我聽說你們打算最近有特賣。

W： Yes, next month. Don't miss it!

是的，下個月。千萬不要錯過它！

M： Could you tell me what items sells the cheapest?

你能告訴我哪些最便宜嗎？

W： Everything is on sale. I can't exactly tell what is cheaper.

東西都在打折。我不能確切地告訴你哪些比較便宜。

M： I can't buy everything. I wish I could know something.

我不能甚麼都買。我希望我能知道一些消息。

W： Why? What if you don't need those cheaper things?

何必呢？萬一你不需要那些便宜的東西呢？

34. M： Look! They have already put those on sale items on line.

看！他們已經將那些特賣的物品公布在網上了。

W： Oh yeah! There are lots of other things on sale.

哦，是的！有很多其他東西特價。

M： I think these dresses may also please you.

我想這些衣服也可以合你意吧。

W： You can say that again, and their seasonal collection is an even more refreshing change from the last season.

說得好，而且他們的當季組合更是比上季令人耳目一新的變化。

M： But these refreshing collections are not on sale.

但這些令人耳目一新的組合不打折。

W： Whatever, it just triggered my sense of shopaholic.

不管怎樣，它就是觸發了我的購物狂感覺。

DAY 3 WEDNESDAY

下面我們繼續延伸上一節的英檢的簡短對話延伸練習。

35. W：Did you watch "Art and Your Life" on A Max last night?
昨天晚上你看了愛美事頻道的「藝術和你的人生」了嗎？

M：Yes I did. How do you think about the program?
是啊？你對那個節目的看法如何？

W：I like the part about Vincent.
我喜歡關於梵谷的部分。

M：Vincent? What's that about?
梵谷的哪方面？

W：I was impressed by his flaming flowers of bright blaze and swirling clouds in violet haze that reflect in Vincent's eyes of china blue.
我印象深刻的是他明亮烈焰式的火紅花朵，以及他青花藍眼睛中，所反映出紫羅蘭色薄霧中的流雲漩渦。

36. W： Mark, what happened? The meeting has started for 30 minutes. Did you miss the train again?

馬克，發生了什麼事？會議已經開了 30 分鐘。你又錯過火車了嗎？

M： I'm sorry, Jen. My car broke down on the way.

我很抱歉，仁。我的車在路上拋錨了。

W： Since when did you start driving?

你甚麼時候開始自己開車的？

【Day 3】
Wednesday

（延伸參考答案）
播放錄音並複誦 ◖◗ Mp3 052

35. M：you just recited Don McLean's song "Vincent - Starry, Starry Night."

你剛剛背誦了唐麥克林的歌詞「文森 - 繁星滿天的夜晚」。

W：You're right. The Starry Night is an oil painting on canvas. It depicts the view of an idealized village.

你是對的。繁星滿天的夜空是一幅布面油畫。它描繪了一個印象化的村莊視圖。

M：Well, I am more concerned about Don McLean's song. He challenged the idea of turning the picture into music.

嗯，我比較在意唐麥克林的歌。他挑戰了把圖像變成音樂的創作。

W：I know that, and in 1972 the song Vincent reached number 1 hit in the UK and number 12 in the USA.

我知道，這首歌 1972 年在英國達到排行榜第一，美國第12。

36. M： I forgot to tell you that I bought a car last week and I
hardly drive myself until today.

我忘了告訴你上星期買了一輛車，今天之前自己很少開車。

W： How coincident is that the car broke down the first time
you drove it?

這麼巧第一次開車，它就壞了嗎？

M： Well, it just happened.

是啊！事情就發生了。

W： OK! We are looking forward to seeing your new car.

好吧！我們期待著看到你的新車。

37. W： OK, now. We are supposed to leave now. John, pack your bags up!

好了。我們應該現在就離開。約翰，收拾你的行李！

W： Why don't we stay for one more night? It's still early to go home.

我們為什麼不多待一晚？要回家還太早。

W： Yeah, but we are over the budget. We'd better check out before they ask us to.

對，但我們的預算不夠了。我們最好在他們要求之前退房。

38. M: Excuse me, could you tell me how to get to the Taipei 101?

打擾一下，你能告訴我怎樣才能到臺北 101 大樓嗎？

W: Let me see... oh, yeah, you can take MRT and get off at the Taipei City hall station. Then walk for few blocks. You will see the huge building.

讓我看看……哦，是的你可以搭捷運，在臺北市政府站下車。然後走幾個幾條街，就會看到那棟巨大的建築。

M: MRT and get off at the Taipei City Hall station. Then walk for a few blocks. Will see the huge building. Thanks a lot.

搭捷運在台北市政府站下車。然後走幾個街區，就會看見大型建築物。多謝。

W: You're welcome.

不客氣！

37. M：How could we be over the budget? Didn't we set all the budgets before this trip?

我們怎麼會超過預算？我們不是早做好了這次旅行的所有預算嗎？

W：Right, but I just bought some jewelry in the lobby shop that cost all the rest of the money we had, and we can't afford to spend one more night.

沒錯，但我剛在酒店大廳商場買了一些首飾，花光了所有剩下的錢，我們現在沒錢再過一夜了。

M：Alright my dear. You may well do that as it is our honey moon, as long as you think it is worthy!

好吧我親愛的。你可以這樣做，因為這是我們的蜜月，只要你覺得值得就好！

38. M : So, are you taking the MRT, too?

　　　所以，你也要搭捷運嗎？

　　W : Yes, and I happened to get off at the Taipei City Hall station.

　　　是的，我碰巧也在臺北市政府站下車。

　　M : Oh, really? Do you mind me in company with you on this trip?

　　　哦，真的嗎？你介意我和你一起走這一趟嗎？

　　W : No, and would you tell me why you're going to Taipei 101?

　　　不會啊，你可以告訴我為什麼要去臺北 101 大樓嗎？

　　M : Of course, I am on a tour visiting the highest view of the world.

　　　當然，我想去參觀世界上最高的視角。

39. M： What's wrong, Anny? You look frightened.

怎麼回事，安妮？你顯得很害怕。

W： I've just seen a horrible car accident! All the passengers were seriously injured.

我剛剛看到可怕的車禍！所有的乘客都受了重傷。

M： Well, why don't you call the police first?

嗯，你為什麼不先報警？

W： Because the victims have been the policemen!

因為受害者已經是員警了！

40. M：Don't forget our flight tomorrow morning.
別忘了我們明天早上的航班。

W：At 8, right?
是八點吧？

M：Yes. But we have to be there an hour early to check in.
是的。但我們必須提前一個小時去辦登機手續。

W：We shouldn't be any problem. Everything we need for the trip has been packed up.
我們應該不會有任何問題。這次旅行所需要的一切都打包了。

M：Not including the souvenir we ordered from this hotel.
不包括我們從這一家酒店訂購的紀念品。

W：Oh, I almost forgot that. When is the arrival?
哦，我幾乎忘了。貨品什麼時候送達？

39. M：Did you see how the accident happened?

你看到事故是如何發生的嗎？

W：Yes. That's why I'm scared to death.

是的。這就是為什麼我嚇得半死。

M：Don't be nervous. You'll do fine. What exactly did you see?

別緊張。沒事的。你到底看到了什麼？

W：There were police cars pursuing others cars of outlaws, and they were shooting each other until the police car was wrecked.

幾輛警車追著幾輛歹徒的車，他們彼此開槍，然後警車就失事了。

M：Wow! That must be a thrilling scene to you and it sounds so exciting. It's like a movie.

哇！那一定是驚悚場景，聽來令人興奮。它就像一部電影。

W：Don't play with me. I haven't got over it yet.

別鬧了。我還沒有還魂咧。

40. M : I don't know. You didn't tell me.

Why don't you ask the lobby shop?

我不知道。你沒告訴我。你為何不問問大廳商店？

W1 : You're right. I'll call them now. (Dial the phone) Hello, this is Mrs. Tomson from room 1203 speaking. Can you tell me when my ordered item will be arrived? I ordered it yesterday.

對。我現在就給他們打電話。（撥打電話）你好，我是 1203 號房湯臣太太。能告訴我訂購的貨品到達了嗎？我是昨天訂購的。

【Day 3】
Wednesday

W2 : One moment please. Ah, It has been here for a while, we'll deliver it to your room immediately.

請稍候。啊，它已經到一會了，我們會立即把它送到房間。

W1 : Thank you.

謝謝！

DAY 4 THURSDAY

這一節我們繼續把上一節未練習完的延伸對話做完。

41. W：Hello, is Cindy there?

你好，辛蒂在嗎？

M：No, she's not at her table now. Maybe she will be back in a minute. Do you want to leave a message?

不，她目前不在位子上。也許她會在一分鐘內回來。你想留話嗎？

W：Yes. This is Maggi. Cindy and I are going to a party tonight. Would you please remind her it's a Halloween night? Tell her to remember the make-up.

是的。我是瑪姬。我和辛蒂今晚要參加一個聚會。請你提醒她這是萬聖節之夜好嗎？告訴她記得化妝。

M：All right, Maggi. I'll remind her.

好吧，瑪姬。我會提醒她。

延伸參考答案

播放錄音並複誦 🎧 Mp3 053

41. M： Cindy, Maggie just called to remind you of the party tonight. She wanted to remind you the Halloween's make-up.

辛蒂，瑪姬剛剛打電話來提醒你今晚的聚會。她想要提醒你萬聖節的化妝。

W： I know. I was just went shopping some pirate costumes for the party.

我知道。我就是去採購一些海盜服裝。

M： Oh, is that old scroll stained with coffee in a bottle your invitation? That's awesome!

哦，那個瓶中沾過咖啡的古老卷軸就是你的邀請函嗎？這設計真棒！

W： Yeah, that's her pirate-themed party except too spooky this year.

是的，那是她今年以海盜為主題的晚會，就是太怪異了。

M： Why? You can wear any spooky costume you want without a care in the world! Isn't it?

為什麼呢？你可以毫不在意這個世界而穿任何怪異的服裝，不是嗎？

W： Right, but playing a disgusting zombie pirate is my last option.

沒錯，但是扮令人噁心的僵屍海盜是我最不想要的選擇。

【Day 4】
Thursday

42. M : I heard you were admitted to New York University.
Congratulations!
我聽說你錄取了紐約大學。祝賀你！

W : Thanks. Yes, I'm ready for the Broadway, Times Square,
Seventh Avenue, and all the fancy shows there.
謝謝你。是的我已經準備好去觀賞百老匯、時代廣場、第七
大道和那裡所有超棒的表演。

M : Excuse me—aren't you supposed to get your degree
in two years? How could you make it with all these
hangouts?
不好意思——你不是應該在兩年內拿到學位嗎？你怎麼還能
有這麼多時間閒逛？

W : Oh, don't you remember my project is exactly about
show business?
哦，你不記得我的研究計畫正是有關演藝事業嗎？

43. M: I heard John is applying for a journalism program. He must be dreaming of winning the Pulitzer Prize.

我聽說約翰正在申請新聞學的研究計畫。他一定夢想著贏得普利茲新聞獎。

W: Well, he's always had an ambition of being a press magnate. Remember that he once made a great report for the local newspaper?

是啊，他一直要當一位報界巨頭的志向。還記得他曾經在當地的報紙發表過很好的報導嗎？

M: Yeah! Think about if he made it to run his own newspaper someday!

是啊！想想如果有一天他經營了自己的報業！

【Day 4】
Thursday

延伸參考答案

42. M: I remember, but I thought is it was the same as any other courses in class rooms.

   我記得了，但我認為它和在教室中的任何其他課程一樣。

   W: Not exactly, I study entertainment industry ranging from managers to artists. You can't just sit in an armchair to learn this industry.

   不完全是，我研究的是娛樂行業，包含經理到演出者。你不能只是坐在扶手椅上去瞭解這個行業。

   M: I see. You need an actual field observation to evaluate your theories.

   明白了。你需要具體的實地觀察，以評估你的理論。

   W: You're right this time.

   這次你是對的。

43. W： According to his dream, he will have to be a successful entrepreneur or businessperson to deal with problems in such fields as television networks, film studios, publishing houses, and internet or multimedia companies rather than just newspaper.

根據他的夢想，他必須成為一個成功的企業家或商人處理比報紙更多的事業，兼顧電臺和電視網路、電影製片廠、出版社，及最近互聯網和其他形式的多媒體公司。

M： That requires more skills than news reporting. It doesn't seem practical for him with his sole talent as a journalist.

這就比新聞報導需要更多的技能。以他只有記者的天賦，夢想成為媒體大亨似乎並不實際。

【Day 4】
Thursday

W： Maybe, but where there is a will , there is a way.

也許吧，但有志者事竟成。

44. W: Jason, can you sort these books out for me?

杰森，你可以幫我來整理這些書嗎？

M: Of course, Mendy. How are you going to classify them? I don't know much about librarianship.

當然，曼蒂。你如何分類它們？我不太懂圖書館學。

W: Oh, that's my job. All you have to do is to stack them by different returned dates.

哦，那是我的工作。你只須要按不同還書日期把它們堆在一起就好。

M: Maybe we can arrange some shelves with returning dates for people to return books.

也許我們可以安排一些標示還書日期的架子讓人們還書。

W: That's a good idea. I'll put some shelves in the hall later.

這是一個好主意。我稍後會在大廳裡放一些架子。

45. M: I just saw an amazing job in the newspaper.

　　我剛在報紙上才看見一個了不起的工作。

　W: Oh yeah? What does it say?

　　哦？它說什麼？

　M: Well, the salary is far higher than my last position, and they offer a car for transportation.

　　薪酬遠遠高於我的上一個職位，並提供一輛代步車。

　W: Sounds good. Where is it located?

　　聽上去很好。它位於哪裡？

【Day 4】
Thursday

　M: Downtown, near your office.

　　在市中心，靠近你的辦公室。

　W: Wow. That sounds too good to be true. How much is the salary? 哇。那聽起來不太真實。薪水是多少？

　M: It's $80,000 a month.

　　一個月 8 萬美元。

　W: $80,000 a month! That's twice of mine! Watch out for the fraud!

　　一個月 8 萬美元！這是我的兩倍！提防欺詐！

延伸參考答案

44. M： Are you a collection development librarian?

    你是編目圖書館員嗎？

    W： Yes, I am.

    是的，我是。

    M： What do you actually do?

    你實際上都做些什麼？

    W： I monitor the selection of books and electronic resources and create profiles that allow publishers to send relevant books to the library. Then I can see those books when they arrive and decide if they will become part of the collection or not.

    我負責選擇圖書和電子資源，並建立檔案，讓出版商把相關的書送到圖書館。當那些書到達時，決定是否藏書。

45. M : I heard some cases of employment fraud. Is that what you
mean?

我聽說一些求職陷阱案件。是你所說的意思嗎？

W : Exactly, it's an attempt to defraud people who are seeking
better jobs by giving them a false hope of better position
with higher wages just like your case might be.

正是，它企圖詐騙正在尋求更好工作的人，給他們一個空的
希望，能得到更好、更高的薪水，可能就像你的情況。

M : Are there promises, such as easy work, high wages for
unskilled labor, and flexible hours?

它的承諾有簡單的工作，不必具備熟練技能、彈性上班時間，
而工資還很高嗎？

【Day 4】
Thursday

W : Now you got the picture.

現在你弄清楚了。

　　我們練習過英檢與多益題型後，也嘗試一題托福形式的簡短對話聽力測驗。先練習聽力作答後，再進一步自己延伸對話。

1. What are the people mainly discussing?

   A. Having enough facilities

   B. The company' money problems

   C. Getting money from an employee activity fee

   D. An activity for the organization

2. What kinds of programs will the student activity fee pay for?

   A. Scientific research

   B. A painting program

   C. Art galleries, play grounds and dancing halls

   D. A new organization program

3. Why do the two employees want to get some of the money?

   A. To make film

   B. To start an arts and crafts fair

   C. To do displays for their painting club

   D. To do modern dance performances

答案：

1. C　2.C　3.C

現在我們看看對話內容：

請聽錄音作答 ◖ ◗ Mp3 054

M：We don't have enough facilities for fun at the the science park. Why can't we have more art galleries, play grounds, and dancing halls?

我們科學園區沒有足夠的娛樂設施。我們為什麼不能有更多的藝術畫廊、遊戲場和歌舞廳？

W：You're right. But do you know about the new employee activity fee?

你是對的。但你知道新員工活動費嗎？

M：No, What's it about?

不知道，是什麼意思？

W：Well, it means more budgets for things like that.

這意味著更多這類活動的預算。

M：You are saying that our painting club will really get any of the budgets, are you?

你該不是說我們的繪畫俱樂部真的會得到一些預算，是嗎？

W：Well, it could.

是的。

M : How?

如何得到？

W : Well, I checked out the company website. They're giving $800 to each registered employee organization. So, if it's not already, we should get our painting club registered. Then, we can ask for $3,800 more after that with another special program!

我查過公司網站。他們對每個已登記的員工組織給 800 美金。所以，如果尚未登記，我們應該為我們的繪畫俱樂部註冊。然後，我們可以以另一特別活動企劃申報 3,800 美金！

M : Wow! What are we waiting for? What exactly is the web site?

哇！我們還在等什麼呢？到底是什麼網站？

W : It's the Apple Activities Park. In fact, they're looking for employee organizations right now.

是蘋果活動公園。事實上，他們現在正在徵募雇員社團。

M : Really! Why do they have so much money?

真的！他們為什麼有這麼多錢？

W：Well, every new employee at our company pays $20 into the fund. It started this month. That wouldn't be too much money for the coming years, so our CEO put in more money. It comes from other programs at the company.

是這樣的，我們公司每一位新員工入支付基金 20 美金。募款這個月開始。但錢在未來的幾年不夠用，所以我們的執行長投注更多的錢。錢來自公司的其他企劃。

M：Oh, I see. So we can do some exhibitions for our painting club! Remember that we were thinking of expressionist art display?

哦，我明白了。所以我們可以為我們的繪畫俱樂部舉辦展覽會了！還記得我們一直想辦的表現主義藝術展嗎？

W：Yes, of course! That's why I was checking on the website!

當然！這就是為什麼我一直在查網站！

托福線上測驗 (IBT) 的聽力測驗共考 34 題，包含 2 段對話，每段五題，4 段講課或討論，每段 6 題。對話的場景多半是校園生活裡（宿舍、餐廳、教室、圖書館）同學間，同學與教師、教師間、圖書館員間、職員間的對話。每段對話都固定有系統的針對內容的主旨大意 (main idea)、論據 (supporting ideas)、推論 (inferences)；說話者的目的、方法、態度來出題，所以對話的內容比較長。現在大家試試再延伸這一段對話。

延伸參考答案

播放錄音並複誦 🎧 Mp3 055

M：You know? We have problem of collecting membership fee. Were you able to find the solution?

你知道嗎？我們收會員費有問題。你能找到的解決方案嗎？

W：We were successful when we started the painting club until we failed to display their works to the public. I think now we have some steps of the solution after we found the funds for the club. First, members need to realize they need a stage after all. Many of them found that they got less, even no chances to display their works after they left the club. It takes time to find a stage, and now it's easy to expect. Second, we need more fun parties for our members, so they can share their experiences of creativity. By doing so, they could find even more satisfaction than displaying art works in a cold gallery. Then, they wouldn't complain about missing a stage because they could have already been on a stage.

我們剛創立繪畫俱樂部時很成功，但當我們未能向公眾展示他們的作品後就有了問題。我認為現在為俱樂部找到經費後，我們的解決方案有幾個步驟。第一，成員需要瞭解他們畢竟需要一個舞臺。許多人發現他們離開了俱樂部之後反而較少，甚至沒有機會去展示他們的作品。找到一個舞臺需要時間，而現在比較容易期待得到了。第二，我們需要更有趣的聚會，讓我們的成員可以分享他們創造力的經驗。這樣，他們會比在一個冰冷的畫廊展示藝術作品更能找到滿足感。然後，他們就不會抱怨缺少一個舞台，因為那樣他們可能已經感覺在舞臺上了。

M : Wow, it sounds like a great plan of yours. Are you sure they will be as eager for a party as for a gallery?

哇，這聽起來像你的一個偉大計畫。你肯定他們會像期待一家畫廊一樣渴望一次聚會？

W : We should be more aggressive promoting our new ideas. We talk with them about the new plan and see how they think. People with a strong passion for painting will express their opinions.

我們應該積極一些去推動我們的新想法。跟他們討論這項新計畫，看看他們的想法。那些對繪畫有強烈感情的人會表達他們的意見。

M: So when do we start to carry on?
所以我們甚麼時候開始去做？

M: After we get the money.
我們得到錢之後。

WEEK 3

簡短談話篇

WEEK **3** 簡短談話篇

在看圖與問答方面都做了結合看圖與問答模擬測驗口說的延伸練習，接下來我們再把範圍擴張到簡短談話（獨白）的聽說練習。先練習聽力測驗後，再分析整段談話的主旨大意與重要細節，延伸下一步自己進行較長篇幅的整段獨白能力。我們先以全民英檢中高級的聽力第三部分簡短談話（獨白）練習題，然後分析這些題型分別要求聽者理解內容的是大意還是細節。

請聽錄音 🎧 Mp3 056

Part C

In part C, you will hear several short talks. After each talk, you will hear 2 to 3 questions about the talk. After you hear each question, read the four choices in your test book and choose the best answer to the question you have heard.

1. A. She made a great fortune from a fund.

   B. She made an impressive waitress.

   C. She saved Afro-Americans' lives.

   D. She gave her money to a charity.

2. A. She's Afro-American.

   B. She's a scholar from Africa.

   C. She never wanted to retire.

   D. She worked in a bank.

3. A. His patient.

   B. His partner.

   C. A supplier.

   D. A waiter.

4. A. Some lessons.

   B. Calling him back.

   C. A new equipment.

   D. Expecting a long time.

5. A. Express understanding and agreement.

   B. Make the necessary phone call.

   C. Describe exactly how it works.

   D. Finish his work as soon as possible.

6. A. To explain the rising risks of texting.

   B. To warn listeners of a dangerous driving.

   C. To describe a new way of texting.

   D. To compare different kinds of text messages.

7. A. Its risk.

B. Its style.

C. Its trend.

D. Its economic value.

8. A. Down the hallway.

B. Next to the lobby.

C. The recreation room.

D. The censor gate.

9. A. Take the students upstairs.

B. Let the students read magazines.

C. Pick up some shoes from the coffee table.

D. Demonstrate the dormitory's sensor system.

10. A. Three days

B. Four days

C. Six days

D. Seven days

11. A. $ 6

B. $ 8

C. $ 10

D. $ 12

12. A. They can buy one and get one free.

   B. They can have a further 15% discount.

   C. They can get 10% off their next purchase.

   D. They can get a free 10-color-pan.

13. A. To introduce an actor

   B. To introduce an actress

   C. To introduce a movie

   D. To introduce a book

14. A. A man

   B. A woman

   C. A teenage boy

   D. A teenage girl

15. A. A best actor award.

   B. A best actress award.

   C. A best director award.

   D. A best music award.

答案

1. D   2. A   3. C   4. C   5. B   6. B   7. A   8. A   9. D   10. A
11. C   12. B   13. C   14. A   15. A

做完「簡短談話」（獨白）聽力練習後，我們除了整段聽力理解之外，還要延伸這段「簡短談話」（獨白）內容分析，以便自己也能做簡短談話的練習。前章我們延伸測驗對話內容，繼續自編對話練習。那麼這一章我們就要延伸為整段的（獨白）練習了。

上一章我們分析「簡短對話」內容，以問題的三類：主旨大意題、細節題、推論題。這一章「簡短談話」（獨白）題型也是這三類。各種題下面就以各篇所測的這三類題目來分析他們的文章結構。確認哪一題是主旨題之後也就掌握了文章主旨，才能有效延伸這個故事，而其他的細節、論據則是新故事可以斟酌增減的參考。這一節我們先以前兩篇談話為範例，分析其主旨、細節後再延伸新的談話。其餘四篇留待下節則由讀者練習自行發揮延伸談話。

問題 1-2 談話內容：

Ms. Mary Delson is an Afro-American woman living in New Jersey. She has been working for over 60 years as a waitress. The day when she retired, she surprisingly found that her monthly pittance had made over $100,000 savings. Then even greater surprise for people, she gave away most of her savings to a charity fund for African-American students. The press highlighted her kindness.

女士瑪麗道森是住在新澤西的黑人女子。她一直從事服務生的工作有六十多年。一天，當她退休了，她驚奇地發現她所儲蓄每月微薄的工資已累積了十萬美元。更為人們驚奇的是，她捐出大部分積蓄給非裔美國人學生的慈善基金。新聞界大幅報導了她的善行。

Question number 1: What did Ms. Mary Delson do that
made her famous?

問題 1：女士瑪麗道森做了甚麼讓她成名？

Question number 2: What did the reporter say about
Ms. Mary Delson?

問題 2：記者報導了甚麼有關瑪麗道森女士的事？

問題 1 的範圍涵蓋了整個完整的內容，是主旨題，也就是說他的正確答案：D. She gave her money to a charity.「她把錢捐給慈善機構」就是這篇短文的主旨。而第二題則是其中一個細節，考驗聽者是否掌握唯一正確的資訊「答案 A：她是非洲裔美國人」。那麼我們若要延伸這個故事，就可以從他捐款這件事再延伸下去若單從她是非洲裔美國人這件小事上，就發展不出甚麼重要的故事了。下面，我們以這一篇的主旨「把前捐給慈善機構」延伸新的談話。

參考答案

請聽錄音 🎧 **Mp3 057**

When Ms. Mary Delson was interviewed by the press, she was estremely humble. As an Afro-American woman living in New Jersey, her only dream was to take Afro-American history at university, but at her age then, she said, her dream would come true by helping young black generations with their education. She saw a need to develop an appreciation for the historic and cultural heritage of African Americans. Just about the same time, she retired with a decent sum of money, she learned the Afro-American Historical Society Museum was in need of donations for further development of the historical and cultural African American exhibitions and programs for scholarships. "What a coincidence to me and this solicitation," she said, "and what am I waiting for?"

當瑪麗道森女士接受記者訪問時，她對她的慈善活動輕描淡寫。身為一位住在新澤西的黑人女性，她唯一的夢想是要在大學裡，學習非洲裔美國歷史，但以她當時的年齡，她說，她的夢想已經透過幫助年輕黑人一代的教育而實現了。她認為有需要發展對非洲裔美國人的歷史和文化遺產的欣賞。就在她退休的同一時間有了這麼一筆錢，她得知美國黑人歷史學會博物館需要捐款，以進一步發展非洲裔美國歷史和文化的展覽和獎學金計畫。「這簡直是對我和這個需求的一大巧合」，她說：「那我還在等什麼」？

問題 3-5 談話內容 ⬤ Mp3 058

2.

Hello, Mr. Brown, the message is from Dr. Johnson. I had my assistant call you back yesterday, but I haven't heard your reply since then. Now I'm personally giving you the message because we do have excellent news for you. The point is that the hospital is going to budget $one million for your surgical table. It appears to be good for operations in the areas of the chest, abdomen, gynaecology, obstetrics, and orthopaedics. You've been promoting this project for more than a year. It's now paid off, congratulations! We are expecting your further presentation about the new equipment. Please contact us soon!

你好，布朗先生，這是強生醫師的留言。昨天我讓我的助手給你回電話，但到現在為止，我還沒有聽到你的回覆。現在我親自給你消息，因為你所關心的事可能會有好消息了。就是醫院將編一百萬美金預算採購你的手術枱。它在胸部、腹部、婦科、產科及骨科部門的測試都似乎良好。你推動這一方案一年多了。現在終於得到報償了，恭喜！我們期待您對新設備進一步展示報告。請儘快跟我們聯繫！

Question number 3: Who is the speaker talking to?

問題 3：說話者對誰說話？

Question number 4: What is the speaker mainly talking about?

問題 4：說話者主要在談論什麼？

Question number 5: What does the speaker want the listener to do now?

問題 5：說話者要聽者現在做什麼？

問題 4、5 是本談話的主旨，4 問「談甚麼」→答案 C.「一個新器材」(A new equipment) 和 5 問「要做甚麼」→答案 B.「打一通必要的電話」(Make the necessary phone call)，因此延伸的談話就須優先以此主旨開頭。其次問題 3 問「對象」→答案 C.「一位供應商」(A supplier)，

當然延伸談話就不能不涉及。下面參考的延伸談話就順著電話留言的情境，也就以電話回覆留言為情境較為貼切。

參考答案

請聽錄音

3.

Hello Dr. Johnson, this is Mr. Brown calling as requested. I'm excited to hear the news. Since you are anxious to learn how the surgical operation table works, I'll give you a preliminary briefing. It is a device including one, a master that detects movement of a body of an operator. And Second a slave that performs surgery on tissue by movement of the operator. The information is supplied from the master, and the slave holds a surgical appliance on an area. This is what I'm going to present in your board meeting. Call me if there are any other questions.

　　強生醫師你好，我是布朗先生依您的要求回電。聽到您的消息很高興。既然你急於想要瞭解外科手術桌如何操作，我將給您初步的簡報。這個設備包括（一）、主控台探測操作員的動態（二）、從動裝置透過主控台的指令執行對人體組織的手術。從主控台發送訊息給從動裝置，從動裝置操作外科器具對身體部位進行手術。這就是我準備在你們的董事會會議中提出的報告。如果有任何其他問題，打電話給我。

DAY 2 TUESDAY

我們接著上一節其他四段談話的延伸練習。

問題 6-7 談話內容

Good morning! It's seven o'clock news report from TNN. For those parents who are listening to our program, how are your children going to school now? Are they riding a motorcycle? The big questions are, are they texting and riding, and are you texting and driving? Today's news included a statistics on the risk of driving and texting. It's 23 times more likely to crash at texting and driving, let alone texting and riding. You may think it is incredible texting and riding, but it just happened 2 hours ago. Two teenagers rode a motor cycle while texting each other before they both crashed in critical conditions.

早上好！現在是 TNN 上午七點的新聞報導。請問那些正在收聽我們的節目的家長們，你們的孩子們現在搭甚麼去上學？他們正騎著摩托車嗎？一個大問題是，他們是一邊發簡訊一邊騎車嗎？而您現在是一邊發簡訊一邊開車嗎？今天的新聞給您開車同時發短信風險的統計資料。開車同時發簡訊有比正常多 23 倍出車禍的高風險，更不用說騎車同時發簡訊了。也許您認為騎車同時發簡訊是令人難以置信的，但那就在 2 個小時前發生了。兩名青少年騎一輛摩托車同時互相發簡訊，結果出了車禍而性命垂危。

Question number 6: What is the speaker's purpose?

問題 6：說話者的目的是什麼？

（答案 B. To warn listeners of a dangerous driving. 警告聽眾危險的駕駛。）

Question number 7: What aspect of texting does the speaker emphasize?

問題 7：說話者強調發簡訊的哪些方面？

（答案 A. Its risk. 它的危險性。）

問題 6 的問答是主旨，問題 7 是細節。試就前一節讀過的延伸範例做一段延伸的談話。

【Day 2】Tuesday

參考答案

請聽錄音 Mp3 060

In this accident, there was a collision with two motorcycles. The witness said the riders of the motorcycles were texting and not paying attention to the road, and as a result they crashed into the gutter by the road. With that the motorcycles were completely smashed in the front and almost completely twisted. The motorcycles were in pieces. The names of these two persons are still unknown, and the policemen are trying to identify them with their mutilated bodies. These riders were stupid because they were texting while riding. Their lives ended because of the stupid mistake they made, even if they had done it many times before.

這是一次兩輛摩托車相撞的事故。目擊者說摩托車騎士一直發簡訊,並沒有注意到路上,結果他們撞進了路邊的陰溝裡。這事故使那兩輛摩托車頭全毀,車身幾乎完全扭曲。摩托車撞成碎片。這兩個人的名字是仍然未知,員警正試圖辨識他們殘缺不全的軀體。這些車手是愚蠢的,因為他們在騎車的同時同時發簡訊。即使他們已經做了很多次這種蠢事,終究因此愚蠢的錯誤結束了生命。

問題 8 - 9 談話內容

OK, students. Let's begin today's dormitory tour with the facilities. As here we are, this is the lobby with TV set and magazine shelf. Please do not bring the magazines to your room or rest your shoes on the couch and coffee table. If you need to do the laundries, we have four coin-operated washing machines and driers down the hallway. We also have a recreation room next to the lobby with two table tennis settings. The most important thing living here is to check in through the censor gate with your student card. You can't get in without matching your fingerprints and the card on the scanner. Please follow me and I'll show you how it works.

好，同學們，我們開始今天宿舍設施的參觀。我們所在的地方，是設置電視和雜誌架的大廳。請不要把雜誌帶到您的房間或把鞋子放在沙發和茶几上。如果你需要洗衣，我們有四個投幣式洗衣機和烘衣機在走廊盡頭。在大廳旁邊我們還提供有兩個乒乓球桌的娛樂室。住在這裡最重要的事情是用你的學生證通過感應大門。沒有經過掃描器上驗證你的指紋和學生證相符，你是進不來的。請跟我來，我會告訴你們如何操作。

Question number 8: Where should a person go if he needs to do laundries?

問題 8：如果一個人需要洗衣，他應該去哪裡？

（答案 A. Down the hallway. 走廊盡頭）

Question number 9: What is the speaker going to do now?

問題 9：演講者現在要做什麼？

（答案 D. Demonstrate the dormitory's sensor system. 展示宿舍的感應器系統。）

這兩個問題都是細節，主題是 "dormitory tour with the facilities" 宿舍的設施參觀。延伸的話題就必須還是宿舍設施介紹，不過問題 9「接下來要做甚麼」倒是必然的話頭。試延伸這段談話。

參考答案

請聽錄音 🎧 Mp3 061

[Day 2] Tuesday

For the new registered students, go to the Office of Student Residence website for **"the password to dormitory gate."** For those who have applied for a password, here are the following tips: first, enter your student ID number and the last four digits of your birthday, then press your fingers on the censor for the prints. Second, to enter the dormitory, enter the password you applied into the door card reader by the gate. Last but not least, the password can only be used for the dormitory the student is residing in.

對於新的註冊學生中，請上學生宿舍辦公室網站找「宿舍大門的密碼」。對於那些已經申請密碼的人，這裡有以下步驟：第一，輸入您的學生證號碼和你的生日最後四個數字，然後按上你的手指以感應指紋。第二，要進入宿舍，在門口讀卡器輸入你所申請的密碼。最後一點重要的是，密碼僅可用於學生居住的宿舍。

問題 10 - 12 談話內容

Shoppers, may I have your attention, please? We're having a happy mother's day sale this week. Over 1,000 items are marked down to just 10 dollars each. There are various pans, irons, kettles, toothbrushes, pastes, and jars at this price. If you're a VIP card holder, you can enjoy a further 15% discount. These sales are amazing, aren't they? You don't want to miss out on this great opportunity, do you? These great deals won't last long. There are three more days left. Grab what you need while you can. Happy shopping!

來賓們，請注意。這一週我們推出快樂母親節特賣。一千多件商品折價只賣 10 美元。有各式鍋具、熨斗、水壺、牙刷，牙膏及瓶罐都是這種價錢。如果你是 VIP 持卡人，你還可以享受進一步 15％折扣。這樣的特賣夠驚人吧？你不會想錯過這個大好機會的！這些大減價不會持續太久，只有三天。盡情搶購吧！購物愉快！

Question number 10: How much longer will the sales last?

問題 10：特賣持續多長時間？

（答案：A. Three days 三天）

Question number 11: What is the price of each marked down item?

問題 11：每項的價格是多少？

（答案：C $ 10 十美元）

Question number 12: What benefit can VIP card holders enjoy?

問題 12：VIP 卡持卡人可以享受哪些好處？

（答案：B They can have a further 15% discount. 享受進一步 15 ％ 折扣）

　　這三題也都是細節，其主旨應該是 We're having a happy mother's day sale this week. 這一週我們推出快樂母親節特賣。因此延伸談話必須還是談特賣會，試做延伸談話。

參考答案

請聽錄音 🎧 **Mp3 062**

Don't you love a good shopping trip on Mother's Day? We're enjoying all the Disney's show at happy mother's day website, so we're celebrating with a sale! Give your Disney's baby wearing hobby a boost with a new wrap, just in time for Mother's Day! Take $60 off wrap orders of $120 or more and $120 off $225 or more! Which wraps have you had your eye on? Hurry up, or the wait is over! Remember, that this sale only qualifies for the new woven and stretchy wraps. This sale will run through Sunday, but for the best selection, shop soon!

母親節那天你不愛一個好的購物之旅嗎？我們欣賞著母親節快樂的網站上的迪士尼表演，所以我們要以特賣慶祝！給你迪士尼寶寶穿著愛好，只在母親節那天，進一步推出了新的尿布！訂購 120 美元以上的可省 60 美元或訂購 225 美元以上可省 120 美元！你中意哪種尿布？快點，否則活動就要結束了！請記住，這次僅特賣新型編織和彈性的尿布。這次特賣到週日為止，好貨有限，要買要快！

問題 13 - 15 談話內容

The Stranger is one of the best movies I've ever seen. It's based on the famous book *The Lonely Woman In the Village* by Martha Roberts. The movie starts with the divorce of a woman in a village following a cheating man's affair with a girl next door. As the story proceeds, all the man and girl's families move away from the village. As a result, only the divorced woman and man left as neighbors. One day, the man shows up in her front yard. Will she change her mind to accept him? Or does the man mean to come back? The ending is quite surprising. Julia Lopez, who plays the woman in this movie, is excellent in the role. Certainly, the movie would not be successful without William Smith, the leading actor. He is in line to win a best actor award because of this movie. Overall, it'll definitely be one of the hits this summer. Don't miss it.

【Day 2】Tuesday

「陌生人」是我見過的最好的電影之一。它是瑪莎‧羅伯茨的名著「孤獨的女人在鄉村」所改編。劇情開始是一個村莊裡的女人，因一個男人與鄰家女孩外遇而離婚。接著，男人和女孩所有的家人都搬離了這個村莊。結果，只有離婚的女人和男人留下作為鄰居。一天，那個男人出現在她的前院裡。她會改變主意接受他嗎？還是那個男人要回來嗎？結局是很令人驚訝。朱麗亞‧洛佩茲，在這部電影裡扮演的女人，演得非常好。當然，這部電影若非威廉史密斯這位男主角不會成功。他因為這部電影入圍最佳男演員獎。總體來看，它肯定將會是今年夏天佳片之一，不要錯過它。

13. What is the purpose of this review?

問題 13：這篇影評的目的是什麼？

答案：C. To introduce a movie 介紹一部電影

14. Who shows up in the woman's front yard?

問題 14：誰會現身在女人的前面的院子裡？

答案：A. A man 一個男人

15. What will the leading actor probably win because of this movie?

問題 15：將這位男主角可能因為這部電影贏得了什麼？

答案：15. A. A best actor award. 最佳男演員獎。

問題 13 是主旨題，其餘兩題是細節。延伸時仍然要以介紹本片為主，試延伸這段影評。

參考答案

請聽錄音 ◖ Mp3 063

[Day 2]
Tuesday

The most important interpersonal communication principles exemplify in this movie The Stranger are: First, intercultural communication: the girl's family next door is from a different race. Therefore, her interaction not only with her neighborhood but others in public or school are not friendly. When they move to the village for the first time other neighbors avoid them. Second, self-concept: the girl meets criticism from her friends as to what she is doing with a white man next door she actually calls him sir. She needs a white family to balance her awkward identity, which is exactly made up by the white man with a sense of authority. The man, however, is in a confusion of tiresome marriage, bumps into this accidental sparks of affection out of the other confusion between admiration and safety.

體現在陌生人這部電影裡最重要的人際互動原則是：第一，跨文化的溝通：隔壁女孩的家人是來自不同的種族。因此，不僅是她的鄰居，其他人在公共場合或學校的互動也是不友善的。他們剛搬到村裡時，鄰居躲著他們。第二，自我概念：女孩的朋友們批評她與隔壁的一名白人男子的所作所為，其實，她尊稱他先生。她需要一個白人家庭平衡她尷尬的身份，而正好這樣一位有權威感的白種男人滿足了她。然而，這個人正困惑於厭煩的婚姻中，撞進了這個分不清欽佩還是安全感的情愫裡，偶然的迸出了火花。

DAY 3 WEDNESDAY

　　我們再做一回全民英檢中高級的聽力第三部分簡短談話（獨白）練習題，然後分析這些題型分別要求聽者理解內容的是大意還是細節。

請聽錄音 Mp3 064

Listen to the following conversation

1. A. Introducing a product.

   B. Describing a process.

   C. Explaining a problem.

   D. Explaining how to attend a high school.

2. A. A group of new teachers.

   B. A new accountant.

   C. A new mechanic.

   D. A group of new students.

3. A. Make an application.

   B. Enroll the school.

   C. Graduate from a high school.

   D. Check the admission.

4. A. A quarter later.

   B. An hour later.

   C. Two forty five pm.

   D. Two thirty pm.

5. A. Weather conditions.

   B. A delayed departure from Paris.

   C. Overbook trouble.

   D. An error in the ticket system.

6. A. To explain the decrease of accidents.

   B. To explain the cause of declining drunk driving.

   C. To describe economical programs for drinkers.

   D. To compare different kinds of drinks.

7. A. The economic effect.

   B. The price of drinking.

   C. Its taste.

   D. Its availability.

8. A. At a restaurant.

   B. During a cooking class.

   C. On the radio.

   D. In a department store.

9. A. It's safe to use.

   B. It's just the right size.

   C. Making striking, consistent, normal and strong coffee.

   D. It's on sale this week.

10. A. An introduction to Miyazaki and his career

    B. An introduction to Miyazaki's award-winning films

    C. An introduction to Miyazaki's drawing style

    D. An introduction to Miyazaki's ambition

11. A. In 1941.

    B. In 1997.

    C. In 2001.

    D. In 2010.

12. A. Howl's Moving Castle.

    B. Princess Mononoke.

    C. Spirited Away.

    D. Airplane.

13. A. At the end of a lecture.

 B. On the last day of class.

 C. After a field trip.

 D. At the begining of a presentation.

14. A. Three.

 B. Four.

 C. Five.

 D. Six.

15. A. They digest very slowly.

 B. Their stomach is divided into four sections.

 C. Their intestinal tract is shorter than humans.

 D. They break down food by crushing.

答案：

1. B 2. D 3. C 4. C 5. A 6. B 7. A 8. D 9. C 10. A

11. B 12. C 13. A 14. C 15. C

做完聽力測驗練習後，繼續「簡短談話」（獨白）內容分析，以便自己也能做簡短談話的練習。

Now, we are going to show you how to apply to the school. You should apply for this status if you have never attended college or university before. First, you must earn a diploma from an accredited high school before you enroll at this school. Make sure to check our admission standards and deadlines before you start the application process. Seconds, all applicants use the same application to apply to the school, entering any programs on our campus. Last, after you submit your application and all of your materials, you will usually wait three to five weeks if you have been admitted. Learn more about what happens after you apply, including how to check your admission status.

現在，我們為你們展示如何申請這間學校。如果你從未上過大學，你應該申請這個資格。首先，註冊前你必須有認可的高中畢業學歷。請務必在開始申請作業之前確認我們的錄取標準和期限。其次，所有申請人都按照相同的申請程序入學，進入我們的校園裡的任何學程。最後，您提交您的申請和所有資料後，如果你被錄取，通常要等待三到五個星期。請查詢更多關於申請之後的手續，包括如何查詢你的入學狀態。

Question 1: What is the speaker doing?

問題一：說話者在做什麼？

Question 2: Who is most probably listening to the talk?

問題二：誰最有可能在聽這次談話？

Question 3: What is the first thing the listener has to do?

問題三：什麼是聽者第一件必須做的事？

【Day 3】
Wednesday

問題一是主旨（答案 B. Describing a process「描述一個程序」）。問題二（答案 D. A group of new students「一群新生」）。問題三（答案 C. Graduate from a high school.「高中畢業」）是細節。因此延伸談話的主題就不能脫離者這個主旨。

參考答案

請聽錄音 🎧 Mp3 065

Welcome! Our school offers all categories of highly ranked academic and professional degree programs, and we encourage talented students from throughout the United States and abroad to apply. The school seeks students who can benefit from its wealth of academic and cultural opportunities. The committee offer admission to those applicants who have the highest potential to succeed in graduate study and who are most likely to have substantial impact on their chosen field. We value our graduate students as important participants in the scholarship and research conducted at this school.

歡迎您！我們學校提供各式各樣排名優異的學術和專業學位課程，而且我們鼓勵美國本土和海外各地的優秀學生申請。本校學生可以從其豐富的學術和文化的教育機會受益。招生委員會給予這些有最大的潛力的申請人入學許可，在研究生階段的學習中取得成功，這些人也最有可能對他們所選擇的領域產生大的影響。我們非常重視我們的研究生來參與這所學校重要的學術和研究工作。

接下來做問題 4、5：

Hello. Passengers of flight FA112 bound for Paris, with stops in Rio De Janeiro. It's two thirty pm local time. The departure gate has been changed to 40B. Also, there will be a slight departure delay due to severe weather outside. The ground crew is in the process of deicing the wings in preparation for departure. It also looks like the flight is slightly overbooked, so we are offering complimentary round-trip tickets to a few passengers willing to take a later flight. We should be boarding about a quarter to three pm. Thank you for your patience.

【Day 3】
Wednesday

你好。飛往巴黎經里約熱內盧 FA112 航班的旅客們。現在是本地時間下午兩點半。登機門已改 40B。此外，因外面天氣惡劣，起飛將稍微延遲。地勤人員正在為機翼除冰以準備起飛。而且本班機的機票也稍微超售了，所以我們向願意改搭晚班飛機的乘客贈送免費來回機票。我們應該可以在下午 2:45 開始登機。謝謝你們的耐心。

Question 4: When should the passengers board now?

問題四：何時乘客該登機？

Question number 5: What caused the problem?

問題五：是什麼導致這個問題？

這兩題都是細節（4. C Two forty five pm.「下午 2:45」5. A Weather conditions.「天氣狀況」），這一段的主旨是「班機延誤資訊」(Flight Delay Information)。因此延伸話題還是延誤資訊。

參考答案

請聽錄音 Mp3 066

Ladies and gentlemen, welcome on board Flight FA112 with service from San Francisco to Paris. The flight scheduled for 2:45 was delayed till 3 pm but now rescheduled to 4 pm. We are sorry for your inconvenience. We are expected to take off in approximately seven minutes time. Please fasten your seatbelts at this time and secure all baggage beneath your seat or in the overhead compartments. We also ask that your seats and table trays are in the upright position for take-off. Please turn off all personal electronic devices, including laptops and cell phones. Smoking is prohibited for the duration of the flight. Thank you for choosing USS Airlines. Enjoy your flight.

各位女士，先生，歡迎搭乘從舊金山飛往巴黎的 FA112 班機。原定下午 2:45 飛行時間推遲到了下午 3 點但現在改到下午 4 點。我們很遺憾您的不便。我們預計將在大約七分鐘的時間起飛。請在這個時候繫好安全帶，確保所有的行李都在你的座位下面或者頭頂的行李架。我們也要求你的座椅和桌子托盤置於直立的位置，以便起飛。請關掉所有的個人電子設備，包括筆記型電腦和手機。飛行期間禁止吸煙。感謝您選擇 USS 航空公司。祝旅途愉快。

問題 6-7

Welcome to the evening report. Today is Friday, a necessary getting drunk evening, but are you driving now? Drunken driving incidents have fallen 40 percent in the last six years, and last year was at their lowest mark in nearly three decades, according to latest national report. The decrease may be due to the down economy: Other research suggests people are still drinking as heavily as in years past, so some may just be finding cheaper ways of imbibing than by going to bars, night clubs and restaurants. "One possibility is that people are drinking at home more and driving less after drinking," said Dr. Theodore Frank, director of the Institute of Accident Control and Prevention.

歡迎收聽晚上新聞。今天是星期五，一醉方休的夜晚，但你現在開車嗎？根據最新的國家報告，醉酒駕駛事件在過去的六年中，下降了 40%，在近三十年來，去年是最低的紀錄。可能是由於經濟低迷而造成紀錄降低。另一項研究表示，人們仍然像過去一樣的暢飲，所以有些人可能是找到比到酒吧、夜總會和餐館更便宜的方法。事故防治研究所主任希多爾‧弗蘭克博士說：「一種可能性就是較常在家裡喝以及較少於喝酒之後駕駛」。

Question 6: What is the speaker's purpose?

問題六：說話者的目的是什麼？

Question 7: What aspect of drunk driving does the speaker emphasize?

問題七：說話者強調醉酒駕車的哪些方面？

　　問題六是主旨（答案 B. To explain the cause of declining drunk driving.「解釋醉酒駕駛紀錄下降的根本原因」）。問題七是細節（答案 A. The economic effect.「經濟影響」）。

【Day 4】
Thursday

參考答案

請聽錄音 Mp3 067

Now let's look at the latest report, a New York mother was responsible for a deadly car accident that killed herself and four children in her car and three men traveling in another vehicle. When the toxicology reports came out, the mother's blood alcohol level was 0.2 percent, nearly two times the legal limit for drivers.

The national studies show that the abuse of alcohol has been increasing among women. Moreover, while driving under the influence arrests has decreased over the past ten years for men, it has increased in women. In fact, the government statistics show that driving under the influence arrests among women was increased by almost 30% in women when comparing 1998 with 2008.

現在讓我們看看最新的報告，一名紐約母親的致命車禍造成了她和四個孩子喪生，遭波及的另一輛車三名男子也喪生。毒物報告顯示，母親的血液酒精含量是 0.2%，近法律限制的兩倍。國家的研究表明酗酒事件一直在婦女當中增加。此外，雖然過去十年男人因酒駕遭逮捕的數字有所下降，但婦女的數字卻已增加。事實上，政府統計數字顯示，1998 年與 2008 年比較情況下，逮捕婦女酒駕數字增加了將近 30%。

問題 8-9

Hello, shoppers. Do you buy expensive coffee because it's too much trouble to make it yourself at home? Well, here's a machine that will save your money. It's called the Extrapresso coffeemaker. It is capable of making striking, consistent, normal and strong coffee. Let me show you how it works. First, Grasp the filter cup and pull it straight out. Insert a standard coffee filter into the cup. Scoop one to two tablespoons of ground coffee per cup of coffee that you want to brew. Insert the filter cup back into its mount. Remove the glass carafe from the plate. Then fill it with water. Use the markings on the side as a guide. Add an amount of water in line with the amount of coffee you added. Last, re-insert the glass carafe onto the plate. Plug the machine in and press the "On" switch located on the side. The Extrapresso begins heating the water and brewing the coffee. Buy this Extrapresso coffeemaker and start saving money on coffee today!

【Day 4】Thursday

你好，買家們。你們買昂貴的咖啡，是因為自己在家煮太麻煩嗎？嗯，這裡有一款機器可以幫你省錢。它是 Extrapresso 咖啡機。它能夠煮出優質、品質穩定、和常見的香濃咖啡。讓我告訴你它是如何操作。首先，取出濾杯並拉直。在杯子裡插入標準的咖啡濾網。每一杯咖啡舀一至兩湯匙的咖啡粉。再把濾杯放回杯座。從壺座取玻璃水壺。然後把它裝滿水。參照側邊的標記。按您所放咖啡粉的量添加適量的水。最後，把玻璃水瓶重新放回壺座上。機器插上電，然後按側邊「打開」鈕。Extrapresso 咖啡機就會開始燒水煮咖啡。買 Extrapresso 這款咖啡機，今天就開始省咖啡錢！

Question 8: Where is this talk most probably being given?

問題八：這次談話最有可能在哪裡？

（答案 D. In a department store.「在一家百貨公司」）

Question 9: What is a special feature of the Extrapresso coffeemaker?

問題九：Extrapresso 的特性是甚麼？

（答案 C. Making striking, consistent, normal and strong coffee.「煮出優質、不變、和常見的香濃咖啡」）

這兩題都是細節，主旨是 "Describing operation process of a machine." 「描述一個機器的操作程序」。因此延伸話題就可以這一篇的結構去談其他的機器操作程序。

參考答案

請聽錄音 Mp3 068

OK, follow me and I'll show you how to operate the photo copy machine.

First, inspect the original documents. Remove staples, paper clips or binder clips holding pages together. Smooth excessively wrinkled or folded pages.

Second, insert the original documents face up into the automatic document feeder. The feeder mounts directly over the plate glass or just to the side on the top of the copier. Third, press the number keys to select the number of copies you want. Fourth, Press the "Start" button on the control panel or the "Start" soft key on the touch display to begin the copy process. Last, remove the copies from the output tray after the copy process has finished. Remove your originals from the automatic document feeder.

【Day 4】Thursday

好吧，跟我來讓我教你如何操作影印機。首先，檢查原始檔案。去除各種裝訂原稿的釘書針、紙夾或長尾夾。撫平過度捲曲或折疊的紙頁。第二，將原稿面朝上插入自動進紙器。進紙器將紙張直接送入玻璃印版或就是在影印機頂端的側面。第三，按數位鍵來選擇你想要的副本數目。第四，按控制台上「開始」按鈕或按觸摸顯示幕「開始」的軟鍵就可以開始複製。最後，在複製過程完成後，從輸出紙盒中取出副本。最後，從自動進紙器中取出您的原件。

問題 10-12

Hayao Miyazaki is the great anime director of fantastic films like *Spirited Away* and *Howl's Moving Castle*. He is always serious about making good anime, often working extra as a writer for the anime he directs.

Born in 1941, Miyazaki loved drawing airplanes as a boy. After he saw a first ever colored animation when he was in high school, his interest in anime grew and he started drawing people as well. Influenced by his mother, who loved questioning common ideas, he creates characters that have surprising and unique qualities. In 1997, the film *Princess Mononoke* made him really famous. It achieved great popularity in Japan, and it was his first film to be sold to the West. Afterwards, he made *Spirited Away*, which broke box office records in 2001 and received many awards, including an Oscar for Best Animated Feature.

宮崎駿是偉大的幻想動畫片導演,以「千與千尋」以及「霍爾的移動城堡」為代表。他總是認真製作好的動漫,常常為他導演的動漫做額外的寫作工作。

宮崎駿生於 1941 年,幼時愛畫飛機。當他在高中的時候,他第一次看到彩色動畫,他就對動漫的興趣增長,他開始畫人物。他受他母親的影響,喜愛質疑社會理念,因此創造的人物也有驚人獨具的特質。1997 年，電影「魔法公主」使他一炮而紅。在日本極受歡迎，這是他第一部賣到西方的電影。之後，他發表了「千與千尋」，打破了 2001 年的票房紀錄，得到了許多獎項，包括奧司卡最佳動畫長片。

Question 10: What is the main focus of this talk?

問題十：這次談話的重點是什麼？

（答案 A. An introduction to Miyazaki and his career「宮崎駿和他的生涯簡介」）

Question 11: When did Hayao Miyazaki became really famous?

問題十一：宮崎駿是什麼時候變得一炮而紅？

（答案 B. In 1997）。

Question 12: Which film of Hayao Miyazaki's broke the box office record?

問題十二：宮崎駿的哪一部電影打破了票房紀錄？

（答案 B. Princess Mononoke.「魔法公主」）

問題十是主旨，十一、十二是細節，以此主旨與細節架構，我們也可以嘗試對其他人物的生涯介紹。

【Day 4】
Thursday

參考答案

請聽錄音 Mp3 069

Claude Monet is a famous French artist as well as one of the founders of the Impressionism art movement of the 1870s and 1880s. The art movement got its name from one of Monet's paintings, Impression, Sunrise. Monet was inspired by the Realists in his early twenties. He loves nature and loves to paint in the fresh air. But rather than depicting the real world in a naturalistic way, Monet observed variations of color and light caused by the daily or seasonal changes. For each person, there is no unchanging landscape that exists independently of our perceptions. We can only perceive the important thing, which would change from moment to moment as the air and light continually changing the surroundings and atmosphere. He thought it was these changing conditions that influenced the subjects of the art with their only true value.

克洛德‧莫內是一位著名的法國藝術家，以及 1970 和 1980 年代的印象主義運動的創始人之一。印象主義運動之名源自於莫內的畫作《印象，日出》。莫內二十多歲時受現實主義者的啟發。他喜歡進入大自然在新鮮的空氣中作畫。但他並不以自然的方式描繪真實世界，而是觀察日常或季節性變化引起的光與色的變化。從每個人的角度看，沒有不變的風景，獨立存在於我們的感知之外。只有人們自己才能察覺到重要的事物，會在每個時刻，隨著空氣和光不斷改變環境和氣氛而改變。他認為就是這些不斷變化的條件，是充滿藝術主題唯一真正的價值。

問題 13- 15

All right, to wrap up, because different animals use their digestive systems in different ways, a variety of digestive systems are required in the animal kingdom. Followings are different examples. One, sloths: with slow-moving nature, his digestive system can take up to a month to process his food. Two, cows: A cow's stomach is divided into four sections. The first section softens the cow's food, the second section sends the food back up to the mouth where it can be rechewed, the third section removes the moisture from food and the last section mixes the food with digestive juices. Three, dogs: dog's intestinal tract is shorter than a human's, due to the amount of protein dogs consume. Four, whales: they have a three-sectioned stomach. The first section of a whale's stomach breaks down its food by crushing. The second section mixes the food with digestive juices and the third further mixes the food and digestive juices. Five, birds, its two-chambered stomach mixes the food with digestive acids and crushes the food thoroughly.

【 Day 4 】 Thursday

好吧，總結是，因為不同的動物以不同的方式使用它們的消化系統，在動物王國需要各種消化道系統。以下是不同的例子。一、樹獺：緩慢的特質，他的消化系統可以用到一個月來處理他的食物。
二、牛：牛胃裡被分為四個部分。第一部分軟化食物，第二部分將食物送回口中反芻，第三部分從食物中移除水分，最後一部分混合消化液與食物。第三，狗：由於大量的蛋白質消耗，狗的腸道是比人短。
四、鯨魚：他們的胃有三個部分。鯨胃的第一部分磨碎分解食物。第二節混合食物與消化液然後第三部分進一步混合食物和消化液。五、鳥類，其雙腔胃混合食物與消化酸液然後完全磨碎食物。

Question 13: When was the talk most probably given?

問題十三：何時最有可能發表此談話？

（A. At the end of a lecture.「在講課的結尾」）

Question 14: How many examples did the speaker just mention?

問題十四：演講者提到多少例子？

（C. Five.）

Question 15: What does the speaker say about the digestive system of dogs?

問題十五：說話者談到狗消化系統的哪方面？

（C. They consume more amount of protein than human do.「他們比人類消耗較多的蛋白質」）

問題十三是主旨，十三、十四是細節，於是可以一段講述同一類事務裡的差異比較為延伸話題。

参考答案

請聽錄音 🎧 Mp3 070

There are a variety of petroleum alternatives available for cars. They were developed because of soaring gas and diesel prices. A handful are being explored and aren't as widely available on today's market. For example, ethanol is a fuel made from plant materials, often wheat or corn. As such, it is a renewable fuel source for cars and is considered an option for environmentally friendly vehicles. Others like biodiesel are typically made from vegetable oils like corn and canola. These are usually considered a renewable resource because they are made from plants. They are also two of the leading fuel alternatives considered by environmentalists.

【Day 4】Thursday

　有很多種用於汽車的石油替代品，因高漲的汽油和柴油價格而發展。少數正在開發而目前市場上並未推廣。例如，乙醇是一種由植物材料製成的燃料，通常是小麥或玉米。如是，它是一種汽車的再生燃料來源而可為環保型汽車的替代燃料。另一種典型用玉米和油菜籽油製造的是生質柴油。由於它們是由植物製成，通常可視為是一種可再生資源。它們也是環保主義者認為是一種優先的替代燃料。

最後這一節我們再以多益的 "Short Talk"「簡短獨白」選 9 題練習聽力測驗，然後繼續練習延伸「簡短談話」（獨白）內容分析，以便自己也能做簡短談話的練習。

請聽錄音 🎧 Mp3 071

Part 4

Directions: You will hear some short talks given by a single speaker. Again, you must answer three questions about what is said in each talk. Choose the best response to each question and mark the letter (A), (B), (C) or (D)on your answer sheet.

Each talk will be spoken only one time and will not be printed in your test book.

Questions 1 and 2 refer to the following talk.

1. What is the talk mainly about?
   (A) Life in United States
   (B) The Brown family
   (C) A family reunion
   (D) Some big cities in the world

2. Which of the following statements about Jim is true?

   (A) He is from German.

   (B) He has no sons.

   (C) Jim works in New Jersey.

   (D) He lives in Canada.

Questions 3 through 5 refer to the following talk.

3. What is the talk mainly about?

   (A) The reason why Adam decided to fly to China

   (B) Some friends Adam was going to meet in China

   (C) A tiring day for Adam

   (D) A flying experience for Adam

4. Which of the following statements about Adam is "NOT" true?

   (A) He was late for the plane.

   (B) He did some shopping at the airport.

   (C) A cab drove him to the hotel.

   (D) He has some Chinese friends.

【Day 51 Friday】

5. What might be the time when Adam went through customs?

   (A) 9 a.m.

   (B) 10:45 a.m.

   (C) 12 a.m.

   (D) 12:45 a.m.

Questions 6 through 9 refer to the following talk.

6. What can be inferred from the talk?

   (A) Samantha's brother is younger than Kevin.

   (B) Kevin had a good time working in a café.

   (C) Samantha and David formed a group before marriage.

   (D) Kevin got a part-time job when he decided to run a business.

7. What is NOT true about Samantha?

   (A) She has long black hair.

   (B) She was 20 when she got married.

   (C) She worked as a waitress.

   (D) She is tall and slim.

8. How many jobs has Kevin had since he was 17?

(A) 4

(B) 3

(C) 2

(D) 1

9. Which food does the group probably "NOT" serve?

(A) Bread

(B) Pizza

(C) Sushi

(D) Chicken wings

答案

1. B　2. C　3.C　4.A　5.D　6.A　7.A　8.B　9.C

問題 1-2

Jim Brown likes his job. He is an engineer. He and his wife live in New York but they are from Canada. They have a big apartment near a park. They have three children. Their names are Tony, Jane and Monica. Mary Brown is a teacher. She works in New York too. She has a car and drives to work. The car was made in German. Jim doesn't have a car but he has a motorcycle. He rides the motorcycle to work in New Jersey.

吉姆布朗喜歡他的工作。他是一名工程師。他和他的妻子住在紐約，但他們都來自加拿大。他們在一個公園附近有一個大的公寓。他們有三個孩子。他們的名字是托尼、珍和莫妮卡。瑪麗・布朗是一名教師。她也在紐約工作。她有一輛車，開車去工作。這輛車是德國製。吉姆沒有汽車，但他有一輛摩托車。他騎著摩托車去紐澤西上班。

Question number 1: What is the talk mainly about?

問題一：主要是在說什麼？

答案 B. The Brown family「布朗家庭」。

Question number 2: Which of the following statements about Jim is true?

問題二：以下陳述中關於吉姆哪一是真的？

答案 C. Jim works in New Jersey「吉姆在紐澤西工作」。

問題一是主旨，問題二是細節，其實就是一個家庭的簡介，這個主旨不改，類似的敘述只要改改人名、職業、工作方式就可以了。

【Day 5】
Friday

參考答案

請聽錄音 Mp3 072

Morgan Stason has a happy family. They live in Taipei. He is an English teacher from Canada, and married with a Taiwanese woman, Miranda. She is an owner of a Cram school. They make a great career together in Taipei city. They have two children. Their names are Teddy, and Maggie. They live in Taipei County and drive about one hour to the cram school every day. The children go to primary school near where their parents work.

摩根斯塔森有一個幸福的家庭。他們住在臺北。他是來自加拿大的一名英語老師，娶了台灣太太米蘭達。她是一家補習班的老闆。他們一起在臺北市經營一個偉大的事業。他們有兩個孩子。他們的名字是特迪和瑪姬。他們住在臺北縣每天開車大約一小時到補習學校。孩子們在他們父母工作地點附近的小學上學。

問題 3-5

Adam flew to China. His plane was scheduled to leave at 10 a.m. Adam made it in two hours to reach the airport and to check in. He arrived at the airport at 9 a.m. He checked in his luggage and went to the duty-free to buy some liquors for some Chinese friends. He boarded the plane at 9:45 a.m. The plane took off at 10:00 a.m. When Adam arrived in Beijing after a 14-hour flight, he went through Immigration and Customs. He took a taxi to his hotel and because he was very tired, he went straight to bed.

亞當搭機飛往中國。他的飛機原定在上午十點起飛。亞當趕在兩個小時內到達機場，辦理登機手續。他上午九點到達機場。送檢行李後，他去免稅店為一些中國朋友買烈酒。他上午 9:45 登機，飛機上午十點起飛。在十四個小時的飛行後抵達北京，他通過了移民機構和海關。他搭計程車到下榻的旅館，因為他很累了，就直接上了床。

【Day 5】
Friday

Question number 3: What is the talk mainly about?

問題三：主要是在說什麼？

答案 C. A tiring day for Adam 「亞當勞累的一天」。

Question number 4: Which of the following statements about Adam is "NOT" true?

問題四：關於亞當以下陳述中哪一「不是」真的？

答案 A. He was late for the plane.

Question number 5: What might be the time when Adam went through customs?

亞當走通過海關的時候可能是幾時？

答案 D. 12:45 a.m.

　　問題三是主旨，其他是細節，循著一定的步驟過程，任何一個勞累的一天都可以發展成故事。

參考答案

請聽錄音 🎧 Mp3 073

On June 2nd, we started the day bright and early by the Hiking at Jade State Park. By 8:00 am we passed the Entry to the state park. After rounding up backpacks filled with water bottles, snacks, sun-block, bug repellent, band-aids, and the camera, we got ready for a day of fun. We planned to hike the 290 acre Jade Lake with 22 miles of trails. They are beautiful paths that weave through forests and open meadows. We wore lightweight pants to protect our legs from brambles and poison ivy. About 12:30, at the end of our hike, there is the boat launch area. We wandered close to the water's edge to skip rocks and toss pebbles. Then, for the rest of the day, we spread blankets on shaded lawn areas for picnic tables and enjoyed a peaceful view of Jade Lake under the shade of many trees with a cooling breeze off the lake. Around 4:00 pm, we had to leave the paradise reluctantly before the sun set. By the time we got home, we were all exhausted with fully loaded memories and went to sweet dream with smiles.

6月2日一大早，我們開始了玉石國家公園一天的健行。上午八點我們進入到國家公園。點齊了滿背包的礦泉水、小吃、防曬霜、驅蚊劑、繃帶、相機後，我們準備好好玩一天。我們計畫遠足 22 英里，圍繞著 290 英畝的玉湖的步道。那些美麗的步道，交織穿過森林與開闊的草原。我們穿著輕便的褲子來保護我們跨過荊棘和毒藤中的雙腿。約中午十二點半，到了我們的終點，泊船區。我們靠著水邊避過岩石，丟著小石漫步。

然後，剩下的時光，我們在陰涼的草坪鋪上毯子，擺上野餐桌，在密林庇蔭與清涼的微風下享受著玉湖畔的美景。大約下午四點，我們不情願地在太陽落山之前的離開這個天堂。回到家的時候，我們滿載著美好回憶而疲憊，帶著微笑而進入夢鄉。

[Day 5]
Friday

問題 6-9

Kevin has his career out of a legendary experience. He left school when he was 17 and took a job as a pizza deliverer. The pay was low so Kevin tried to find another part time job to make extra money. However, life was just not easy for him. He couldn't find any payment elsewhere except the pizzeria. Fortunately, the chef decided to teach him how to make pizza. He learned very well. Five years later, he was a qualified sous chef. In the first year in his new job, he met Samantha, who worked in the pizzeria as a waitress. She was two years younger than Kevin and was tall and slim with shoulder length blond hair. Five months later, they got married. At the wedding Kevin met Samantha's teenage brother. He happened to be a waiter from a diner. The three formed a group and started their own mobile pizzeria. Friends told them that their food was very good and that they ought to think of running their own pizzeria chain. They are now doing very well as a franchise pizzeria holder.

　　凱文經歷了傳奇般的職業生涯。17 歲時，他離開了學校，做一份比薩送貨員的工作。薪水很少，所以試著找其他兼職來賺外快。然而，謀生並非易事。除了比薩店，他找不到其它地方賺錢。幸運的是，廚師決定教他如何做比薩。他學得很好。五年後，他就成了合格的二廚。在這新工作的頭一年，他遇見了在比薩店當服務生的莎曼珊。她比凱文小兩歲，高而苗條披著及肩的金髮。五個月後，他們就結婚了。在婚禮上凱文遇見了莎曼珊正值青春期的弟弟。他碰巧是一家小餐館裡的服務生。三人合作自己考慮開了一家行動比薩店。朋友告訴他們餐點做得很好，他們應該經營他們自己的披薩連鎖店。他們現在做得很好，經營著一個比薩加盟。

Question number 6: What can be inferred from the talk?

問題六：從談話中我們可以推斷出什麼？

答案 A. Samantha's brother is younger than Kevin「莎曼珊的弟弟比凱文年輕」。

Question number 7: What is NOT true about Samantha?

問題七：關於莎曼珊什麼是不真實的？

答案 A. She has long black hair「她有長長的黑頭髮」。

Question number 8: How many jobs has Kevin had since he was 17?

問題八：十七歲之後凱文有過多少就業機會？

答案 B. 3。

Question number 9: Which food does the group probably "NOT" serve?

問題九：他們可能「不」提供哪種餐點？

答案 C. Sushi「壽司」。

問題六是推論題，其他都是細節，主旨是「凱文的傳奇生涯」，因此類似的傳奇生涯都可以延伸。

Wu Pao Chun was brought up by a poor family of eight children, and lost his father at the age of 12. He left home at 17 to Taipei and became a bread apprentice. The life of an apprentice was even harder than his childhood. He was hurt by the burning tray in the arms all the time. Finally, after 4 years hard work, he made a traditional baker. However, the traditional baking was outdated in the market, and Wu's bread was in serious decline in the sales.

At that time, Wu sought comments from a famous self-taught baker, Chen Fu-guang. Chen taught him to cast aside the conventional baking, and redefine the word "delicious", which is the taste of red wine, cheese, French cuisine and delicacies.

With Chen's help, Wu broadened his horizons and even started to learn Japanese in order to read foreign recipes.

Encouraged by friends and business partners, Wu started in 2005 to take part in bakery competitions in Taiwan. His home-grown leaven became his secret weapon. In 2007, he won the Asian bakery championship. The following year, Wu and two other fellow bakers from Taiwan won silver medals in the bread Olympiad's in Paris, France. Wu also won the individual

European bread winner. In 2010, Wu represented Taiwan to participate in the inaugural World Cup in Paris Masters Bread, defeated the other seven country participants, and further won the European-style bread group world champion.

吳寶春在一個有著八個孩子的貧窮家庭長大，12 歲就失去了父親。他 17 歲時離家到臺北，去當一個麵包學徒。學徒的生活甚至比他的童年更艱難。他經常被炙熱的烤盤燙傷手臂。終於經過 4 年的辛勞之後，他成為一個傳統的麵包師傅。然而，在市場中，傳統烘焙方式已經過時，而吳寶春的麵包銷售量嚴重下降。那個時候，吳寶春徵求從著名的自學烘焙師陳撫光的意見。陳教他拋開傳統的烘烤方式，並重新界定「美味」一詞，也就是紅葡萄酒、乳酪、和法國美食的味道。在陳的協助下，吳開闊了他的眼界，甚至開始學日語以研讀外國食譜。在朋友和商業夥伴鼓勵下，吳始於 2005 年參加臺灣的烘焙比賽。他的本土酵母成了秘密武器。2007 年，他榮獲亞洲烘焙冠軍。次年，吳和兩個其他來自臺灣的同胞麵包師贏得在法國巴黎奧林匹克麵包賽銀牌。吳也贏得歐洲個人賽獎。2010 年，他代表臺灣參加在巴黎首屆世界麵包大師盃比賽，擊敗其他七個國家的參賽者，進一步獲得了歐式麵包組世界冠軍。

【Day 5】
Friday

WEEK 4

申論篇

WEEK **4** 申論篇

DAY **1** MONDAY

　　本書開宗明義就指出口說練習與聽力練習是一貫不可分割的。所以本書的設計就以各種英聽測驗的例題作為口說的文本 (context) 與知識範圍，然後針對所測問題作為引導延伸所測驗的文本。從複誦、朗誦、應答、對話、到簡短獨白的談話練習。基本上，這些練習都是「順藤摸瓜」有例可循的練習。到了最後這一章就要讓讀者嘗試在沒有例子的導引下，抒發個人的意見，這類的考驗也為較高級英語測驗的要求，例如多益的口說測驗，表達意見 (Express an Opinion) 是在最後一題，而全民英檢也要到中高級以上的口說測驗「第三部分申述題 (Discussion)」才涉及。不過，正如本書所強調的聽與說的不可分割，我們就不必拘泥於這些測驗的模式，因為本書的主要目的並不是以通過測驗為目的，而是真正有效的訓練出口說能力，當具備真正能力的時候，這些測驗也考不倒你了。我們只是利用這些測驗的文本為範圍，以問題為引導，來練習口說，達到既有益於應考，也有益於實用的目的。

　　「表達意見」與「申述」題設定在較高級的考驗是因為受測者已經具備了初、中級的語言知識，足以獨立表達意見或申述。但就本書循序漸進的過程下，最後這一級的考驗也是不可或缺的。如果以本書為練習一句的學習者還不具備獨立申述的能力，我們還是要以完整的範本讓學者參考才有意義。已經熟練了上一章延伸簡短談話練習的學習者,已可以體會我們所練習以簡短談話聽力測驗問題類型(主旨、細節和推論)的引導,延伸出另一段談話並不困難,所以我們這一章仍然要可以用全民英檢或多益口說的例題引導,不同的是,前兩節先看參考答案,然後分析答案的主題、細節或推論是甚麼,然後書中再以類似的問題,讓大家自己做一篇類似的答案。

以下就以英檢中心所公布的測驗評分標準讓大家參考。

中高級口說能力測驗		
級分	分數	說明
5	100	對應內容適當、切題;說話流利,表達清楚有條理;發音、語調正確、自然;語法正確,字彙使用自如,雖偶有錯誤,仍能進行有效的溝通。
4	80	對應內容大致適當、切題;發音、語調大致正確、自然;字彙、語法尚足供表達,對一般話題能應答自如,使用上仍有錯誤,但不妨礙溝通。
3	60	能應答熟悉的話題;說話雖不太流利,但已具基本語法概念及字彙,有時因錯誤而影響溝通;發音、語調時有錯誤。
2	40	尚能應答熟悉的話題;發音、語調錯誤多;字彙、語法認知有限,語句多呈片段,表達費力,溝通經常受阻。
1	20	僅能應答非常簡單的話題;發音、語調錯誤甚多;語法概念及字彙嚴重不足,表達能力極有限,溝通困難。
0	0	未答 / 等同未答。

資料來源：https://reg.lttc.org.tw / GEPT / Exam_Intro / t03_ introduction.asp

下面就以英檢中心公佈的中高級口說預試題目以及答案先讓大家參考：

Part III   Discussion

Read the questions, think about your answers to the questions for 1½ minutes, and then record your answers for 1½ minutes.

The Internet has become very popular these days. Do you use it? What can we do with the Internet and what problems might it cause? Please explain.

參考答案：

請聽錄音 Mp3 075

I use the Internet every day. With the Internet, I can access desired information instantly. I can find out what's happening around the world in just a few minutes, and I can also get in touch with friends through e-mail, and they can get back to me very quickly in just a few minutes. With the invention of the Internet, the distance between people is less than it used to be. But there are some problems as well. People sometimes post violent or pornographic pictures on the Internet. Young children, who like to browse the Internet, are very likely to see them. In addition, gangsters can use the Internet to buy and sell weapons and drugs without getting caught. These are problems we are not really happy when we see them. Improper uses of the Internet have led to more problems than we can think of. Sometimes these problems are too crippled to cope.

資料來源：https://www.gept.org.tw / Exam_Intro / t03_
　　　　introduction.asp# 題型簡介

譯文

　　我每天都使用互聯網。有了互聯網，我可以立刻取得想要的資訊。我可以在幾分鐘內得知世界各地發生了什麼事。我也可以透過電子郵件在互聯網上聯繫朋友，而他們也可以幾分鐘內給我回覆。隨著互聯網的發明，人們之間的距離比過去短多了。但還有一些問題。人們有時候在互聯網上貼暴力或色情的照片。喜歡瀏覽互聯網的年幼孩童，很可能看到它們。此外，歹徒們可以利用互聯網來買賣武器和毒品而逍遙法外。這些不是我們樂於看到的問題，因為社會被迫要投入大量精力去處理它們。

　　我們分析文本的主旨仍然可以從問題就看出來，就是"What can we do with the Internet and what problems might it cause?"「我們可以用互聯網做什麼以及它可能會導致什麼問題？」這個問題可以與上個問題"Do you use it?"相關也可以無關，不過你不能以為回答"I never use Internet"後面就不必作答了，要知道英檢的評分重點除了上表列出五項之外，「作答量」也是一大重點，如果你的回答只有那麼一句，當然得不到幾分的。這一題命題的目的是希望你能表達自己的經驗，然後提出自己的意見。如果沒有自己的經驗，還是可以從客觀角度提出看法的。因此我們可以從參考答案中看出主旨就是「互聯網可以做甚麼，它可能導致甚麼問題？」從這一點來發揮自己的看法。這樣的延伸，我們再上一章練習了很多，不過不知道大家是否真的發揮出來了呢？如果發揮有限，那就把上一章的參考答案當作暖身的覆誦練習，這一章我們再進一步扎實的分析一篇口說答案所必備的字彙、片語以及基本知識。這種分析可以透過同伴的討論先建立起來，就以上述的問題彼此討論一番，不管你是否使用互聯網，至少可以從互聯網的優缺點討論起，討論時就自然涉及與互聯網有關的詞彙了。

討論互聯網的優缺點，可以先玩猜猜看的遊戲，大家各列出五個好壞處，然後對照看看差別，這就可以蒐集足夠的知識。

Benefits of the Internet 互聯網的好處	Problems of the Internet 互聯網的壞處

　　此表只是格式，內容多少並不因格子大小而受限，儘可自由延伸內容，然後再就各自列出的好壞處進一步解說細節。

參考資料：
Advantages of the Internet 互聯網的好處

1. The most information resources 最多的資訊來源

Accessible information on almost all subject including government law and services, trade fairs and conferences, market information, new innovations and technical support, resources for homework, medicine, and even advice on personal affairs.

2. The best and fastest communication 最好最快的通訊

A. Real-time communication with someone in other parts of the world

B. Video conferencing, chat, and messenger services all over the world.

3. Online Services and E-commerce 線上服務和電子商務

A. Booking tickets for a movie, transferring funds, paying utility bills and taxes without having to leave our homes or offices.

B. E-commerce transferring money through the Internet, reaching over a variety of products and services, such as eBay.

B. Wikipedia, Coursera, Babbel, Archive, and Teachertube, sharing knowledge to people of all age groups.

4. Entertainment for Everyone 人人可得的娛樂

A. Finding the latest updates about celebrities and exploring lifestyle websites.

B. Downloading games either for a price or for free.

5. Social Networking and Staying Connected 社群網站與持續連繫

A Facebook or Twitter staying connected with friends and family, in touch with the latest happenings in the world.

B. Searching and Applying for jobs and business opportunities on forums and communities.

C. Chat rooms meeting new people.

6. Inexhaustible Education 無盡的教育

The World Wide Web (WWW) from the academic, to greater knowledge and know-how on subjects making it possible for homeschooling with videos of teachers just like a real classroom.

Problems of the Internet 互聯網的壞處

1. Personal Information stolen 個資遭竊

Our personal information of internet for banking, social networking, or other services, is often stolen or misused by thieving websites and individuals causing the damage by having our identities misused and our accounts broken into.

2. Spamming 垃圾郵件

Unwanted e-mails serving endless line of advertisements slows the computer system is mixed with our more important emails.

3. Virus attacks 病毒攻擊

Virus programs activated simply by clicking a seemingly harmless link crashes the system completely.

4. Adult Content 成人內容

Pornography and age-inappropriate content, the biggest problem of the Internet, lacking of control over the distribution to children.

5. **Social Isolation, Obesity, and Depression** 社會隔離、肥胖和 抑鬱

A. Confusion between the real and virtual world addicting everything with excessive surfing, online gambling, and social networking creating both physical and mental health complications.

B. Sitting long time in front of the computer and then exercising less cause obesity and depression.

大家交換了所知的資訊以後，各自在表中填入好壞處，然後試著 自己說出互聯網的好壞處。

參考答案

請聽錄音並覆誦 Mp3 076

There are both advantages and disadvantages in the Internet. The benefits are:

First, it has the most information resources accessible on almost all subjects, ranging from government law and services, trade fairs and conferences, market information, new innovations and technical support, resources for homework, medicine, to even advice on personal affairs.

Second, it provides the best and fastest communication.

Third, it has real-time communication with someone in another part of the world and video conferencing, chat, and messenger services all over the world.

Fourth, it has online services and E-commerce, such as booking tickets for a movie, transferring funds, paying utility bills and taxes without leaving our homes or offices, and it has E-commerce transferring money through the Internet, reaching over a variety of products and services, such as eBay. It also has Wikipedia, Coursera, Babbel, Archive, and Teachertube, sharing knowledge with people of all age groups.

Fifth, it has entertainment for everyone to find the latest updates about celebrities and exploring lifestyle websites and downloading games either for a price or for free.

Sixth, it has social networks, such as Facebook or Twitter staying connected with friends and family, get in touch with the latest happenings in the world and has networks searching and applying for jobs and business opportunities on forums and communities. It also has chat rooms to meet new people.

Seventh, it has inexhaustible education, the World Wide Web (WWW) from the academic, to greater knowledge and know-how on subjects making it possible of homeschooling with videos of teachers just like in a real classroom.

互聯網中有利亦有弊。

好處：

一、它擁有幾乎所有學科最多的訊息資源，從政府法律服務作業、貿易展覽和會議、市場訊息、創新和技術支援、藥品甚至個人事務建議。

二、它有最好最快的通信。

三、它與世界各地的人都可進行即時通信、視訊會議、聊天和信差服務。四、它可以訂電影票，轉移資金，支付水電費和稅金，而無須離開我們的住宅或辦公室。還可以透過互聯網，如 eBay 進行電子商務轉帳，取得各種產品和服務。它也有維基百科、Coursera 教育科技公司、巴貝爾、檔案網、和教師視頻，與所有年齡層的人的分享知識。第四，它可以讓大家找到最新的名人動態、探索生活網站的娛樂，以及花錢或免費下載遊戲。

五、可用社群網站「臉書」和「推特」 保持與朋友和家人聯繫，接觸世界上最近發生的事件，在論壇和社區網路還可搜尋申請就業和商業機會。還有聊天室能結識新朋友。

六、它有取之不盡、用之不竭的教育資源——萬維網 (WWW) 涵蓋著從學術到更多的知識和專門技能，可以就像真實的課堂一樣，在家與教師的視頻上課。

請聽錄音並覆誦 🎧 Mp3 077

The problems of the internet:

First, our online personal information for banking, social networking, or other services, is often stolen or misused by thieving websites and individuals causing the problems by having our identities misused and our accounts been broken into.

Second, our computer system may be slowed down by spam e-mails serving endless lines of advertisements the mixing with our more important emails. Third, our system is attacked and completely crashed by virus programs activated simply by clicking a seemingly harmless link. Fourth, our children are exposed to adult content as age-inappropriate pornography as the biggest problem of the Internet, lacking of control over the distribution to. Fifth, excessive surfing, online gambling, and social networking create both physical and mental health complications resulting in social isolation, obesity, and depression.

第二，互聯網的問題：一、我們的在銀行、社交網路，或其他的服務互聯網個人資訊，常常被盜或被竊盜網站，因濫用我們的身份和我們的帳目，造成個人損失。二、我們的電腦系統被垃圾郵件阻塞使得速度減慢，無止盡的廣告混淆了我們更重要的電子郵件。三、只因點擊一個看似無害的連結，我們的系統遭病毒程式啟動攻擊而完全當機。四、互聯網最大的問題，缺乏控制色情的散佈，我們的孩子受到不適合其年齡層所該觀看的成人內容侵襲。五、過度上網、線上賭博，和社交網路，造成生理和心理的併發症而導致社會隔離、肥胖和抑鬱症。

大家是否都作了自己的一段有關互聯網好壞處的申論呢？英檢的測驗時間是 90 秒，但我們練習的重點並不一定要先以此為限，而是盡量放寬自己對這個問題的發揮空間，哪怕只是與同伴閒聊一下這個話題也未嘗不可。只是彼此應互相仔細檢查口說的發音、文法問題，隨時提醒對方，甚至於把對方所說的內容記錄下來，有助於增進自己的聽力。這樣聽與說的互動才是有效的聽說訓練。

這一節我們仍以英檢考題練習一次。

The gap between rich and poor is a big issue nowadays. Do you think the gap between rich and poor in Taiwan is serious? Why? If the government should do something to solve the problem, what would it be?

富人與窮人之間的差距現在是一個大問題。你認為富人和窮人之間的差距在臺灣嚴重嗎？為什麼呢？如果政府應該做些什麼來解決這一問題，它會是什麼？

參考答案
請聽錄音並覆誦 🎧 Mp3 078

I think in the long run, the gap between the rich and poor will become more obvious. Although the measurement of this gap is lower than the international warning line, the survey of family income, we found the gap will be widened in the future.

Causes of the wealth gap associated with globalization, which made financial liberalization, information communication technology progress, trade barriers reduction, the deepening integration of the global economy, the release of the labor force in emerging economies. Besides, in light of technical progress and wage equalization, the low-skilled and unskilled labor tends to be unemployed in the higher technical developed countries, and caused a wage compression. In particular, Taiwan's the main production model, the acting industry or OEM (original equipment manufacturer), made meager profits, repress unskilled workers' wages and expand the uneven distribution of income.

　　我認為長遠來說，富人和窮人之間的差距會更明顯。雖然評估數字顯示台灣的貧富差距指數尚低於國際警戒線，但從家庭收入的調查發現，貧富差距將在未來擴大。

　　貧富差距的成因與全球化有關。金融自由化、資訊通訊科技進步，貿易障礙降低，全球經濟體整合程度日益加深，促使新興經濟體釋出勞動人口。此外，在技術進步及工資均等化效應下，發展程度較高的國家其原有低技術勞工及非技術勞工的工作機會流失，使勞動薪資成長空間受到壓縮。特別是我國主力產業以代工為主的生產模式，利潤微薄，非技術勞工工資受到壓抑，使得所得分布不均的擴大。

　　貧富差距的原因很多，參考答案只說出 90 秒內可以說出的一部分，我們還是可以用一個表去蒐集其他同伴的意見，然後表達自己關心的意見就可以了。重點在於表達是否流暢，用字與結構是否正確。

下表列舉文中相關可以發揮的一些原因：

The causes of the widening gap of the rich and poor 貧富差距擴大的原因	
globalization	
financial liberalization	
information communication technology	
trade barriers reduction	
integration of the global economy	
cheap labor force in emerging economies	
low interest rates	
OEM	
gap between urban and rural development	
Tax cut	

　　此表只是格式，內容多少並不因格子大小而受限，儘可自由延伸內容，然後再就各自列出的好壞處進一步解說細節。

下面再延伸一篇意見表達。

請聽錄音並覆誦 🎧 Mp3 079

After the financial tsunami, funds loose fueled a speculative bubble. Low interest rates, loose monetary environment, resulted in real estate prices and the impact of low-income families. In addition, long-term tax policy tilted to the rich. Tax cuts continued to capitalists, such as the inheritance and gift tax in 2009. Foreign assets were remitted back to Taiwan speculation in real estate, while not importing into the substantial investment to increase employment opportunities worsening a polarization gap. Moreover, public resources are unevenly distributed. More resources are given to the north rather than the south, resulting in a long-term uneven land development. Therefore, the south is suffering from income inequality problems.

金融海嘯後，資金寬鬆助長投機泡沫。低利率、寬鬆貨幣環境造成不動產價格高漲，衝擊中低所得家庭。加上長期向富人傾斜的租稅政策，持續向資本家減稅，如 2009 年大降遺產贈與稅。而海外資產匯回台灣炒作房地產，卻未導入實質投資增加就業機會，造成貧富差距惡化。此外，公共資源分布不均。公共資源供給北多於南，導致國土長期地不均衡發展。因此，南部遭受所得不平的問題。

DAY 3 WEDNESDAY

　　回顧我們上一章以及這一章的延伸口說練習，我們以聽力測驗的題型分析來引導進一步的申論，題型主要分為三類：主旨、論據和推論。這三類也就是答題的依循重點。前兩節我們所練習的兩個主題基本上只用了兩個重點：主題與論據 (topic and supporting) 不過，不知道大家是否就真的能流暢的說出來類似參考答案的內容？若還有距離，我們就須要加強更基本的問答模式練習。這些基本模式還是環繞著主題與論據，以便經過這些紮實的練習後，最後大家還是能夠逐步的掌握表達內容的重點。

練習一、表達主題時，我們可以參考幾個基本的問答模式，找同伴交
　　　　互以這些模式編問答內容：

Question	Answer
They all think A is worse than B. Which do you think is worse?	I think / believe...
Would you prefer A or B?	I would prefer...
Would you rather A or B?	I would rather...
"People usually would..."Do you agree or disagree?	I agree / disagree that...
It has recently been announced that a project will be built. Would you support or oppose the project?	I would support / oppose...
What is your opinion on this issue?	My opinion is...
If you can make an important decision on A or B, which would you do?	If I could choose a decision, I would...
Are you in favor of the school / community's doing?	I am in favor of / I am against...

【Day 3】
Wednesday

參考答案

請聽錄音並覆誦 🎧 Mp3 080

Question and Answer
They all think death penalty is worse than a life sentence. Which do you think is worse?
I think / believe a life sentence is worse.
Would you prefer traveling abroad or in your homeland? I would prefer traveling abroad.
Would you rather swim indoor or outdoor? I would rather swim outdoors.
People usually would choose to eat out on weekend. Do you agree or disagree? I agree that eating out on weekend is good for the family reunion.
It has recently been announced that a project to be built. Would you support or oppose the project? I would oppose because project that will hinder the transportation.
What is your opinion on raising tax on the rich? My opinion is raising tax on the rich would help narrow the gap of incomes.
If you can make an important decision on charging or not charging the U-bike in the first half hour, which would you do? If I could choose a decision, I would charge the U-bike.
Are you in favor of the school / community's doing? I am in favor of the school's policy.

（表中只表達正面或反面一個意見，同學也可以練習另一面的回答）

練習二、回答問題時，複誦問題中的核心部分，那也是主題。

例題：

請聽錄音並複誦 🎧 Mp3 081

Part 2

1. Would you prefer to <u>travel</u> in homeland or <u>abroad</u>?

   Answer: I think I would prefer to <u>travel abroad</u>.

2. Boys learn better in science than girls. Do you agree or disagree?

   Answer: I disagree because <u>boys learn better in science than girls.</u>

3. The municipality will use part of your community as a depot of the refuse truck. Do you support or oppose the plan?

   Answer: I would oppose the plan to <u>use part of your community as a depot of the refuse truck.</u>

　　這三個問題當然也可以回答另一個正面或反面的選擇，複誦的部分是一樣的。

練習三、回答主題之後，接著就要表達自己的論據，以支持自己的意
見。

論據可能很多，這時就須要以表達順序的承轉詞、片語來編排諸
多論點來介紹、增加、總結自己的論據，例如：

請聽錄音並複誦 ◖◗ Mp3 082

Part 3 Listing

First, second, third..., First of all, The first reason is, The
second reason is, The other reason is, Another reason why is,
The final reason is, Also, I also think that, etc.

再以一個例題的回答練習運用這些承轉詞：

請聽錄音並複誦 ◖◗ Mp3 083

Part 4

Would you prefer to study abroad or in your own country?

Answer:

Topic「主旨」

I would prefer to study in my own country.

Supporting points「論據」

The first reason is I would have many troubles with the
language.

Also, I can't get used to the foreign customs.

The final reason is, I couldn't stand with the homesickness when I am alone.

　　做完以上三個練習以後，我們就體驗多益的口說測驗第 11 題，也是最後的申論題 "Express an opinion"「意見表達」。

請聽錄音 　Mp3 084

Part 5

Question 11: Express an Opinion: In this part of the test, you will give your opinion about a specific topic. Be sure to say as much as you can in the time allowed. You will have 15 seconds to prepare. Then you will have 60 seconds to speak.

Do you agree or disagree with the following statement?
Is it better to purchase on websites than through ordinary shops.
Use specific reasons and examples to support your answer.

Preparation time
00:00:00

　　（你同意還是不同意以下聲明？是否在網站上購買比普通商店更好。使用具體原因及實例來支持你的答案。）

參考答案：

請聽錄音並複誦 🎧 **Mp3 085**

I think that it is better to purchase on the website rather than the ordinary shops.

First, incredible convenience: traditional stores operate with fixed hours, while online shoppers can choose any time of the day or night to get on the Web and shop. This is especially convenient for families with small children, or simply in bad weather. Second, price comparisons: you don't have to walk all day "in the market for" the best deal when you visit a website to settle for whatever prices the site has placed on a particular item. Third, limitless choice: shelf space in a traditional store is limited, while on line you can find as various goods as you like. Four, no pressure sales: eager salespeople bug you all the time in a real market, but you don't have to put up with that online.

　　我同意網站上購買比普通商店更好。一，極為方便：傳統商店有固定的營運時間，而線上購物者卻可以選擇白天或晚上的任何時間購物。特別對有年幼孩子的家庭或純粹惡劣的天氣下更是方便。二，價格的比較：你不需要走一天「去尋找」最佳的價錢。當你造訪一個網站，可以決定任何特定的商品，因為所有價錢都已在網站上了。三，無限的選擇：傳統商店的貨架空間是有限的，然而網上你可以找到你所想要的各種各樣的商品。四、沒有採購壓力：在實體市場上，總是有積極的推銷人員打擾你，但網上你不必忍受這種麻煩。

　　本文的立場是支持網購的優點，編排論據的承轉詞是：First, Second, Third...。下面我們再試試表達網購缺點的意見，並試一試其他承轉詞的組織方式。

【Day 3】
Wednesday

參考答案：

請聽錄音並複誦 Mp3 086

Answer 2

I don't like buying goods online.

The first reason is: you can't have a feel about clothes you'd like to purchase. You really need to see how it's made when purchasing a cloth. Even if you are familiar with a certain brand, you can also buy a cloth that's not suitable for you. Sometimes the return policy and shipment are annoying. If you're buying a clothing item, it's impossible to feel the material and see how it's made. Unless you know your sizes and are familiar with the brand of selling clothing, this could end up being a bad experience.

Another reason is that you can't ask someone about the products immediately. If you have a question about the item, you probably will have to wait at least 24 hours to get a question answered.

I am also concerned about privacy and security: privacy and security are desperate concerns for any online shopper. For that misgiving, you need to make sure your transaction is a safe one, install free spyware removal tools, identify online scams and hoaxes, surf anonymously, and keep your Web usage private.

　　我不喜歡上網買東西。第一個原因是，你無法感受到你想要買的衣服。當購買衣服時，你真的需要知道是如何製成的。即使你熟悉特定的品牌，可能還是買到不適合你的衣服。有時後退換貨政策和運送是惱人的。如果你買了一項衣物，卻無法感受到質料且知道是如何製成的。除非你知道你的尺寸而且熟悉所銷售品牌的衣物，否則最終會是個不好的經驗。另一個原因是，你不能立即詢問產品。如果你對商品有問題，你可能會至少要等 24 小時才能得到回答。我也很關心隱私和安全： 隱私和安全是任何線上購物者迫切關注的問題，你需要確保您的交易是安全的，安裝免費的間諜軟體移除工具，查證線上詐騙的侵擾和惡作劇，匿名上網，保持網路使用的私密方式。

DAY 4 THURSDAY

　　上一節我們練習了如何回應問題的主題與論據的編排，最後練習了對一個問題正反兩面的回應模式。也許大家比較習慣回答正面的意見不太善於反面的答覆，但是每人都可能有個人獨特的想法，這也是我們從模仿他人到跳脫範本的第一步。當你覺得可以自由的表達自己想法的時候，我們的特訓不就成功了嗎？而且達到那一步也不是遙不可及的，其實反面意見也是有一些有用的模式可以遵循的，如下：

請聽錄音並覆誦 🎧 Mp3 087

There are many ways to do this, but I think...
有許多方法可以做到這一點，但我認為……

Maybe most people would agree with this, but I...
也許大多數人會同意這一點，但我……

Most of the opinions are in favor of that decision, but if I had a choice, I guess I would say...
意見，大部分都贊成這一決定，但如果我有一個選擇，我想我會說……

Well it's a hard question, but I think the most important thing is...
很好，這是一個困難的問題，但我認為最重要的事情是……

I think there are pros and cons for this issue, but if I had to choose, I would say...

我認為這一問題有正反兩面意見，但如果我不得不選擇，我會說……

由於只是個人意見表達，而不是闡釋真理，這些表達方式就要表現客觀、包容的態度，所以多用假設語氣 "If I had..." "I would..." 這些句型。

下面我們就練習幾個可以表達不同意見的問題。

請聽錄音並覆誦 🎧 **Mp3 088**

1. Some students prefer to live outside of campus near the downtown, shops, restaurants, and entertainments. Other students maintain living in the dormitory where it is quiet and convenient for any study facilities. Which do you prefer and why?

一些學生願意住校園外面，靠近市中心、商店、餐館和娛樂場生活。有些學生仍然願意住在宿舍，那裡安靜而且研究設施都方便。你比較喜歡哪一種，為什麼呢？

2. Some people think teenagers should be taught at school how to raise children of their own, others think that it is their

parent's duty to teach them. What is your opinion and why?

有些人認為學校應該教青少年如何養育自己的孩子，有些人認為去教他們是父母的責任。你有什麼看法，為什麼？

參考答案：

請聽錄音並覆誦 Mp3 089

1. There are many pros and cons to live in or out of the campus, but if I had to choose, I would prefer to live out of the campus where I can temporally stay out of the anxious academic atmosphere as well. My parents like most of the others, are for the campus side though.

   對於住校或校住校外有很多正反意見，但如果讓我選擇，我寧願住校園外面，在那裡我可以暫時遠離焦慮的學術氛圍。但我的父母卻最贊同住校那一邊的意見。

2. There are many things that teenagers equipped themselves for life, and raising children is one of them. My opinion is that schools should be responsible for teaching teenagers some necessary skills of raising children. The main reason is that parents are too busy to remind their children of their

homework or worse, their own business. The other reason is that nowadays to many parents' surprise more and more teenagers get pregnant, and they are totally unprepared for the pregnancy, let alone thinking of teaching them how to raise the baby.

青少年需要學習很多技能來充實自己的生活，而養育子女就是其中之一。我的意見是，學校應負責教導青少年一些撫養子女的必要技能。最主要的原因是父母太忙於他們孩子的家庭作業，或更糟的是，太忙於他們自己的工作。另一個原因是，現在越來越多的青少年在父母的驚訝下懷孕，他們根本未準備好接受懷孕之事，更別說是教孩子如何照顧嬰兒。

前面運用假設語氣練習表達個人不同意見，但是仍需要明確的說出「這是我個人意見」，如：

請聽錄音並覆誦 🎧 **Mp3 090**

In my experience, it is better to major in a subject I like because it is more important to feel happy than to be a student from a famous school.

以我的經驗，修習一門我喜歡的學科比較好，因為感到快樂比成為一位名校學生更重要。

To me, exercising regularly is really important because it helps you stay fit.

對我來說，運動經常是真的很重要，因為它有助你保持身體健康。

The main reason why I think the campus shouldn't be a depot of the refuse trucks is the foul smell they emit have effects on teachers and students.

我認為校園不應該成為垃圾車停放處的主要原因是，它們釋放的臭味影響了教師和學生。

It did happen to me before, and in that case I chose not to tell parents immediately about their children's misbehavior and helped them to tell their parents themselves.

過去它確實發生在我身上，並在這種情況下，我選擇了不立即告訴父母孩子的不當行為，而是協助他們自己告訴他們的父母。

In my family, the problem was a serious once, so I have a good experience to deal with it.

在我家中，這一問題曾經很嚴重，所以我有很好的經驗可以用來解決它。

In my experience, it is always better to stay in a cellar than any other places in a tornado.

以我的經驗，在龍捲風來時，待在地窖裡比其他任何地方都好。

同學可以找同伴以一個問題，練習上述畫線的部分相互問答，例如：

Some people think it is better to buy groceries on sale, others prefer to buy them at an ordinary price. What is your opinion on purchasing timing?

有些人認為在特價時買雜貨比較好，另一些人則主張以普通的價格去買就好。你對購買時機的看法是什麼？

參考答案：

請聽錄音並覆誦 Mp3 091

【Day 4】Thursday

To me, buying on sale is always disappointing because we tend to buy too many unnecessary things.

The main reason why for not buying things on sale is that you might buy too many things you don't really need.

It did happen to me before, and in that case I chose not to buy anything on sale for things mostly at the end of expiry date.

In my family, we don't buy groceries on sale as the market or shopping mall is always crowded and children are overwhelmed by the fatigue while struggling with the crowds.

In my experience, buying groceries on sale is the stupidest thing in life. When we buy a lot of cheap, unnecessary things appearing to be some "trophies" in a battle of rush, we simply spend more money than we tried to save.

中譯

對我來說，大減價時買太多不必要的東西總是令人感到失望的。

不想在大減價時，買東西的主要原因是，你可能會買太多你不真正需要的東西。

它過去確實發生在我的身上，在那種情況下，我決定不去買大減價的任何東西，那些大多已到了有效期限。

我的家人在大減價時不去買雜貨，因為市場或商場總是人滿為患，兒童也不堪人群中擁擠的疲憊。

以我的經驗，大減價時買雜貨是生活中最蠢的事。當我們買很多的便宜而不必要的東西，看起來像是搶購戰場中得來的「戰利品」，其實我們花的錢遠比我們想省的錢還多。

我們練習了上述的反面意見回答模式，其實只是訓練如何表達自己意見，也許你除了想表達自己意見之外還是想採納一些正面的意見，這也是一般人在討論或辯證的過程中自然的反應，所以我們作文時，寫論說文會按「正、反、合」或「起、承、轉、合」四個步驟表達，這就顯得你的表達內容不至於偏頗而更為周延圓滿。因此，我們接下來練習的表達就不只如上述只敘述一個主題和一個論據而已，我們在考慮論據時就要納入與自己不同或相反意見的辯證，最後再把辯證的結果歸納到結論中「合」起來。

這就必須在講話前先擬好大綱：

1. 決定自己對該議題的意見。（例如：贊成或不贊成"agree or disagree"支持或反對"support or oppose"）
2. 想想二至三個主張這個意見的理由。
3. 再想想與自己不同意見的理由，但是確信自己的理由比較重要。
4. 再說一次自己的意見。

接著我們就找一個議題來練習一下大綱。

If you can make an important decision on charging or not charging the U-bike in the first half hour, which would you do?

如果你可以針對 U-bike 公共自行車在前半小時收費或不收費作出重要的決定，你會做何選擇？

1. My opinion: not charging. 我的意見是不收費

2. Supports for my opinion: saving energy and reducing carbon emission. 我的論據：節約能源和降低碳排放量。

3. Other opinion and reasons: users charge but the policy will discourage the exercise activity and increase the carbon emission.

其他意見和理由：使用者付費，但這項政策將抑制體能活動和增加碳排放量。

4. My conclusion: not charging. 我的結論：不收費。

下面我們再以兩個議題來練習一下大綱：

Question one 問題一

Should college students take on a part time job? Why or why not?

大學生應否打工？可或否的理由？

1. My opinion: 我的意見是：

_____

2. Supports for my opinion: 我的論據：

_____

3. Other opinion and reasons: 其他意見和理由：

_____

4. My conclusion: 我的結論：

_____

參考答案：

請聽錄音並覆誦 Mp3 092

1. I don't agree with college students taking on part time jobs.

   我不同意大學生打工。

2. They need to focus on their own academic task, and part time jobs occupied too much their time. Part time jobs may consume too much their energy before they can practice any theories they learn.

   他們必須專注於學業，而打工佔據了太多時間。打工可能耗損太多精力以致根本無法應用所學。

3. Part time jobs help college students apply their theories on practice.

   打工有助於大學生應用所學。

4. I don't think college students should take on part time jobs.

   我不同意大學生打工。

Question two 問題二

Do you prefer shopping in a traditional market or a supermarket? Why?

你比較喜歡在傳統市場或超市購物？為什麼？

參考答案

請聽錄音並覆誦 🎧 Mp3 093

1. I prefer shopping in a supermarket.

   我比較喜歡在超市購物。

2. Supermarket is cleaner. Traditional market is usually wet and nasty with butchering chicken and fish. Supermarket's prices are all fixed. Tricky bargain in a traditional market bothers me.

   超市比較乾淨。傳統市場通常殺魚殺雞的又濕又噁心。超市的價格都是固定的。傳統市場的討價還價使我困擾。

3. Traditional market offers good social occasions for shoppers and venders.

   傳統市場提供了攤商與顧客之間很好的社交場合。

4. I prefer shopping in a supermarket.

   我比較喜歡在超市購物。

　　列好大綱之後，再這些句子用常見表達贊成或反對、對比或比較的句型、連接詞或承轉副詞連接起來。例如：

prefer（比較喜歡）的相關句型：

　　prefer＋N／V-ing＋to＋N／V-ing 比較喜歡⋯⋯而非⋯⋯
＝prefer to＋V＋rather than＋V
＝prefer to＋V＋instead of＋V-ing

例句：
請聽錄音並覆誦 Mp3 094

　　I prefer fast walking to jogging.
＝I prefer to walk fast rather than jog.
＝I prefer to walk fast instead of jogging
　　我比較喜歡快走而不是慢跑

　　另一類似「比較喜歡⋯⋯而非⋯⋯」的句型，在兩者中進行取捨，表示「寧願⋯⋯不願⋯⋯」，「與其⋯⋯寧可⋯⋯」的意思時，可用 **would rather... than...** 或 **would... rather than...** 的句型，例如：

請聽錄音並覆誦 Mp3 095

I would rather shop online than go to the market.
我寧可網購而不願去市場。

The children would swim there rather than sail a bamboo raft.
孩子們寧願游泳去那裏而不願划竹筏。

表達反對、對比或比較的連接詞如：**but, whereas, while, although...**

請聽錄音並覆誦 Mp3 096

Not that I love Caesar less, **but** that I love Rome more.
不是我不愛凱撒，而是我更愛羅馬。

Some praise him, **whereas** others condemn him.
有些人讚揚他，而有些人譴責他。

Hospitals in the south tend to be better-equipped, **while** those in the north are relatively poor.
在南方醫院往往會得到好的裝備，而北部則相對較差。

Although they're expensive, they last forever and never go out of style.
儘管價格昂貴，但它們經久耐用，永不過時。

表達反對、對比或比較的承轉詞如：**yet, however, nonetheless, nevertheless, on the one hand, on the other hand, on the contrary...**

請聽錄音並覆誦 Mp3 097

I don't eat much, **yet** I weigh 90 kg.
我吃得不多，我體重卻有 90 公斤。

Some students failed. **However**, all the girls did quite well.
有些學生不及格。但所有女生的表現都相當不錯。

There was still a long way to go. **Nonetheless**, some progress had been made. 路還很長，不過已經取得了一些進展。

The news may be unexpected; **nevertheless**, it has been confirmed.
這消息可能是出乎意料的，然而，卻已經證實了。

On the one hand, the low oil price makes consumers happy. **On the other hand**, if it remains low, the macro economy may be harmed.
一方面，低油價讓消費者開心。另一方面，如果它仍然很低，宏觀經濟可能受到傷害。

People all say they don't do things like that. **On the contrary**, they do them all the time.

人們都說根本不會做那樣的事情。正好相反，他們一直都那樣做。

做過這些練習，大家對於如何表達反對、對比或比較是否就比較有概念了呢？現學現賣，我們就以前面所做過的兩則大綱，運用這些句型、連接詞與承轉副詞把個別的句子連結起來。

再回顧問題一，以及其四點大綱：

Should college students take a part time job? Why or why not?

大綱：

1. I don't agree with the idea that college students should take part time jobs.

2. They need to focus on their own academic task, and part time jobs occupied too much their time. Part time jobs may consume too much their energy before they can practice any theories they learn.

3. Part time jobs help college students apply their theories to practice.

4. I don't agree with college students taking on part time jobs.

可以把它們整理成下面的完整回答：

請聽錄音並覆誦 🎧 **Mp3 098**

Most people encourage college students to take on part time jobs, but I don't agree with the idea that college students should take part time jobs because they need to focus on their own academic task, and part time jobs occupy too much of their time. However, some people maintain that part time jobs help college students apply their theories to practice. Yet, part time jobs may consume too much of their energy before they can practice any theories they learn. Therefore, I still don't agree with college students taking on part time jobs.

【Day 4】Thursday

大多數人鼓勵大學生擔任兼職工作，但我不同意大學生兼職工作，因為他們需要把重點放在自己的學術任務上，而兼職工作佔用太多時間。然而，一些人主張兼職工作有助於大學生把他們的理論應用在實際工作上。然而，兼職工作可能會在他們可以實習他們學到的任何理論之前消耗太多精力。因此，我仍然不同意大學生擔任兼職工作。

問題二，以及其四點大綱：

Do you prefer shopping in a traditional market or a supermarket? Why?

1. I prefer shopping in a supermarket.
2. Supermarket is cleaner. Traditional market is usually wet and nasty with butchering chicken and fish. Supermarket's prices are all fixed. Tricky bargain in traditional market bothers me.
3. Traditional market offers good social occasions for shoppers and venders.
4. I prefer shopping in a supermarket.

整理成下面的完整回答：

請聽錄音並覆誦 Mp3 099

I prefer shopping in a supermarket because supermarket is cleaner. Nevertheless, traditional markets offer good social occasions for shoppers and venders; but to me, traditional market butchering chicken and fish are usually wet and nasty. Although bargaining in traditional market is a kind of pleasure, that bargain is still tricky and bothers me. I would definitely prefer shopping in supermarket.

　　我喜歡在超市購物，因為超市較乾淨。然而，傳統市場提供購物者和攤商良好的社交場合；但對我來說，傳統市場通常因屠宰雞和魚而潮濕骯髒。雖然在傳統市場中討價還價是一種樂趣，但我覺得討價還價依然太麻煩而使我感到困擾。我肯定比較喜歡在超市購物。

　　練習了大綱的連結後，是否對於整篇的表達更有概念了呢，如果仍然覺得難以啟齒，或者一開始就不知道如何擬大綱，那大家就需要更扎實的去記誦一些引導式套語，如本節一開始就讓大家練習了五句套語來引導自己的意見，再回顧一次大綱第一段：

For me, ... I feel, ... I reckon, ... If you ask me, I ought to...

The main reason I think...I'm convinced that... I've always held that...

It did happen to me before, and in that case ...

In my family, ...In my country... From my point of view, ...

In my experience... In my view... In my opinion.. I maintain that...

　　其實大綱第二段，對表達自己立場提出論據上，也有一些套語來表達各式依序舉例，如：

For example, ..., For instance, ... Let me give an example...

First of all, ... Second, ... Third, ...

Everyone knows that... It's common knowledge that...

One of the reasons, ... According to experts... One

researcher claims that...

Also, a very important factor... It's a fact that... One important statistic is...

第三段「轉」為對比或比較的套語，這類就是本節練習的重點，表達反對或反面意見：

Yet, I don't think...
However,... Nevertheless, ...
On the one hand... On the other hand...
On the contrary...

第四段總結自己的主張：

All things considered I would ...I would prefer this, ...So I would...
All in all,...
I still think...
Overall, I would say...

這些都是一開始覺得難以啟齒應答的時候，可以用來引導回應的套語，你可以把這些套語背熟，一經引導，就可以慢慢想出一些應答了。

【Day 4】
Thursday

DAY **5** FRIDAY

這一節我們再把上一節所有的應答技巧,包括擬定大綱、運用連接詞及承轉詞連結大綱、運用套語引導應答等,再做統整的練習。第一個問題我們先看參考答案,然後大家試做擬定大綱、運用連接詞及承轉詞連接大綱、運用套語引導應答等的分析,第二個問題我們再試著自己從大綱、連結、引導整合成自己的答案。

Question 1 問題一

Due to a recent air crash in the middle of the city, public opinion is shifting. People are in favor of moving the airport. Do you support or oppose the opinion? Why?

由於最近在市中心的空難,輿論正在轉向支持搬遷機場。你支持還是反對這意見?為什麼呢?

請聽錄音並覆誦 🎧 Mp3 100

I would support the opinion to move the airport away from the center of the city.

First of all, with the recent accident as a warning sign, the frequent ascent and descent of the aircraft poses a potential threat to citizens' life. Also, while the city is developing with a more and more population, some residents inevitably suffer from a huge noise. As the urban development grows, the large amount of land an airport requires becomes a barrier space to progressing constructions.

On the other hand, one of the biggest benefits of erecting the airport in the center of a city is the convenience. People living near the airport have enjoyed the convenience and profits they bring. Also, this has opened more business opportunities for businessmen and the pleasure for travelers. After all, the city has the nature of transportation center which makes the best use of an airport. Meanwhile, it is a big business and would create lots of jobs for local people.

That being said, I would still prefer to travel further to an airport than to have one close to my house.

中譯

我會支持機場搬離城市中心的意見。首先,最近發生的空難事故是一個警訊,頻繁的上升和下降的飛機構成了對市民生命的潛在威脅。此外,隨著這城市發展的增長,一些居住在航道下的居民無可避免地承受巨大噪音。隨著城市的發展不斷增長,機場所需的大量土地成為建物擴張的障礙空間。另一方面,在市中心建造機場最大好處之一是便利性。居住於機場附近的人已享受所帶來的方便和利益。畢竟,城市具有運輸中心的性質,使機場得以充分運用。同時,它還是一筆大生意,可為當地居民創造大量就業機會。雖然說了這麼多,我還是寧願去遠方,而不去一個在我家附近的機場。

首先分析大綱：

1. **My opinion...** 我的意見是……

   I would support the opinion to move the airport away.

2. **Supports for my opinion...** 我的論據……

   a. The recent accident posed a potential threat to citizens' life.

   b. Residents living under the course suffered from the huge noise.

   c. The land of an airport became a barrier to urban development.

3. **Other opinion and reasons...** 其他意見和理由……

   a. The convenience for people flying for business and pleasure.

   b. A city makes the best use of an airport.

4. **My conclusion...** 我的結論……

   I would still support the opinion to move the airport away.

其次找出「比較喜歡……」的句型：

I would support the opinion...

找出表達反對、對比或比較的連接詞或承轉詞：

While, On the other hand,

找出對比或比較的套語：

Having said that, I would still support ...

下面我們就讓大家自己針對一個題目，先做上述的大綱、連結與對比表達準備，然後整理出自己的回答。

Question 2 問題二

Some people admire innovation, and they take up a challenge against the tradition. Others like to stay with routines and don't want to make any change. Which attitude do you prefer? Explain your reason.

有人崇尚創新，挑戰傳統。其他人喜歡保持現況並不想做的任何改變。你比較喜歡哪一種態度？解釋你的原因。

【Day 5】
Friday

參考答案

一、大綱：

1. **My opinion...** 我的意見是……

I would adopt the attitude of innovation.

2. **Supports for my opinion...** 我的論據……

Innovation brings us new ways of life.

Innovative involves challenges and risks defying the tradition.

Challenge broadens our horizon of reality and develops different strength and talents creating a better world.

Bill Gates dropped out of Harvard creating his outstanding technology career and a brand new information world.

3. **Other opinion and reasons...** 其他意見和理由……

We like opportunities under guaranteed security.

Following the routines of Harvard, Gates could easily find a steady job.

4. **My conclusion...** 我的結論……

I would adopt an innovative attitude to life

二、連結用語：

預備「比較喜歡⋯⋯」的句型：

I would adopt an attitude...

預備表達反對、對比或比較的連接詞或承轉詞：

On the other hand... but

預備對比或比較的套語：

Having said that, I would prefer to...

三、完成答案：

請聽錄音並覆誦 🎧 Mp3 101

I would adopt an attitude of innovation and new ways of life.

Innovation brings us new ways of doing things, building things and new ideas to change the world we got used to, so being innovative involves challenges and risks defying the

【Day 5】 Friday

tradition. Challenge broadens our horizon of reality improving our present life. Challenging tradition allows people to develop different talents creating a better world. For example, Bill Gates dropped out of Harvard for more innovative Microsoft, not only creating his outstanding technology career but also a brand new information world for human beings. Quitting Harvard must be the hardest choice to make for any student, but Gate's courage of taking that step eventually paid off.

On the other hand, we like opportunities under guaranteed security that comes with knowing what will happen. Following the routines of Harvard, Gates could easily find a steady job after graduated. Betting ones most promising education on a risky business is the last decision for most of us to make.

Having said that, I would prefer to have some adventure just like what Bill Gates had, so I would adopt an innovative attitude to life.

中譯

　　我會採取創新和新生活方式的態度。創新帶給我們做事情、建構事物的新方法和改變我們所習慣世界的新想法，所以創新意味著各種挑戰和冒險以顛覆傳統的新方法。挑戰拓展了我們的現實視野，改善我們目前的生活。挑戰傳統讓人們開發不同的才能以創造一個更美好的世界。例如，比爾‧蓋茲從哈佛大學退學去開發更具創新性的微軟，不僅為自己創立了卓越的科技事業，更為人類開創了一個全新的資訊世界。離開哈佛對任何學生勢必是最難的選擇，但蓋茲勇於踏出那步最終得到的回報。

　　從另一角度看，我們喜歡的機運是保證安全而可預知情事的。遵循哈佛的常規，畢業後蓋茲能很容易找到一份穩定的工作。把最有前途的教育做為賭注，壓於高風險的事業上，對我們大多數的人來說，是最不該做的決定。

　　話雖如此，我寧願要一些就像比爾‧蓋茲一樣的冒險，所以我會採取創新的生活態度。

　　要提醒大家的是，以上的作業程序是我們練習口說的思考程序，並不是寫作練習，大家還是要注意自然口語表達的發音、音調、用語等等，一如本書開始時所要求大家注意的。然而語言的學習本是聽說讀寫一氣而成，不可分割的。聽與說的能力自然也與讀與寫的能力不可分割，如果大家仍覺得口說能力不足，那就勢必要在閱讀與寫作上再加功夫了，也許我們可以期待下一本書「寫作特訓」出版時再會了。

WEEK **1** 回答問題篇錄音稿

 DAY **1** MONDAY

MP3 001

Question 1: What is he doing right now? (15" pause)

    a. He's eating lunch.

    b. He's taking a bus.

Question 2: What is your favorite place to spend free time? Why? (15" pause)

    a. My favorite place is 228 Memorial Park because the trees and flowers are beautiful.

    b. My favorite place is Chiang Kai-shek Memorial Hall because it has the best theater in the city.

Question 3: How old were you when you first went abroad? Why? (15" pause)

    a. I first went abroad when I was twenty-two. I went to the States to study.

    b. The first time I went abroad was when I twelve to learn English in England.

Question 4: In some places we shouldn't smoke. What are some of these places? (15" pause)

    a. We shouldn't smoke in any public places.

    b. We shouldn't smoke at any places with No-

Smoking signs.

Question 5: What would you do if the fire alarm set off while you were watching a movie? (15" pause)

a. I would rush to the exit immediately.

b. I would stay seated and wait for the instruction to leave orderly.

Question 6: When is the time that you feel energetic? in the morning, the afternoon, or the evening? Why? (30" pause)

a. In the morning because I usually sleep early and well.

b. In the evening because I am really relaxed after work.

Question 7: Why do some people say that it isn't good to eat out nowadays? What do you think? (30" pause)

a. Sanitation of foods is the main concern for most people, and because of the tented oil problems nowadays, some people think it might not be a good idea to eat out. I think it's a loophole in the food security standards.

b. People are afraid of the problematic food sources; even the famous fast food chain imports expired food from food suppliers.

Question 8: Do you feel happy easily? What might be some good ways to be happy? (30" pause)

    a. Yes, I do feel happy easily. My way to be happy is to feel content all the time. When you can sleep well, eat well, or get along with people well, it's kind of great.

    b. No, I don't feel happy easily. My way to be happy is trying to be in other's shoes and find out why they don't like me.

Question 9: Have you done something interesting last year? Tell me about it. (30" pause)

    a. Yeah, I traveled to California. I visited Universal Studios to see how movies are produced and I had a lot of fun.

    b. Yes, I volunteered to teach English in the remote villages in the Tai Dong county. I found teaching those children is so meaningful to me.

Question 10: Would you rather travel to China or the U. S.? Why? (30" pause)

    a. I would rather travel to China because languages, foods, and customs are all suited for my tastes.

    b. I would rather travel to the States because I want to learn English in an authentic language surrounding.

MP3 002

I.

1. The snow melts away in spring.

2. Still water runs deep.

3. Day breaks. Day dawned. It breaks.

4. Every minute counts.

5. The food can't keep.

6. He doesn't fit in.

7. The work doesn't pay.

8. It depends.

9. I may return very soon.

10. He goes abroad tomorrow.

MP3 003

II.

1. Seeing is believing.

2. He looks very happy.

3. He seems naïve.

4. The streets appeared messy.

5. Don't make him appear a beggar.

6. He remained silent.

7. Please keep quiet.

8. After the struggle, he became rich.

9. He went happy.

10. His face turned blushed.

MP3 004

III.

1. I like him.

2. They need love.

3. They want to go swimming.

4. He thinks that the movie is good.

5. He enjoys talking to girls.

6. We cannot help laughing.

7. I don't mind closing the window though it's very hot.

8. The company is considering changing the policy

9. Hope keeps us alive.

10. Wealth enables men to be courteous.

11. It starts to rain.

12. It starts raining.

MP3 005

IV.

1. The teacher asked the little girl to stand up.

2. I heard him singing when I walked in.

3. We elected Tom (to be) the representative.

4. We chose him to be the leader of the group.

5. They made him a worrier.

6.We call him "The Father of the Republic."

7.His parents named him Tom.

8.I found the movie very interesting.

9.I believe that heis a good teacher.

10.Keep your mouth shut.

11.Please make yourself at home.

MP3 006
V.

1. Kevin gave me a pen.

2.Sue lent me a book.

3. He bought me a map.

4.I forward my friends an e-mail.

5. He offers me lots of information.

6. She read me some famous articles.

7. I can find her the lost diamond.

8. My girlfriend made me a pie.

9.I asked him a question.

10.He told me a joke.

11.He did a trick to us.

12.I hold a grudge against him.

13. He threw the cat a stone. = He threw a stone to the cat.

14. He threw the dog a bone. = He threw a bone to the dog.

DAY 3 WEDNESDAY

(Narrator):Questions 4–6: Respond to questions

Directions: In this part of the test, you will answer three questions. For each question, begin responding immediately after you hear a beep. No preparation time is provided. You will have 15 seconds to respond to Questions 4 and 5, and 30 seconds to respond to Question 6.

(Narrator): Imagine that you are participating in a research study about allergy. You have agreed to answer some questions in a telephone interview. (Beep sound)

MP3 007

Question 4

What kinds of allergic symptoms do you, your family members, or friends have? (Beep sound)

MP3 008

Question 5

What kinds of allergic symptoms do you, your family members, or friends have? (Beep sound)

MP3 009

Question 6

What allergens cause those symptoms of you, your friends, or your family members? (Beep sound)

Suggested answers

MP3 010

Question 04

In summer, my <u>mother gets allergy</u> in air-condition rooms for a long time.

<u>I</u> usually <u>suffer</u> from allergy when seasons change.

My <u>father is allergic</u> to seafood and milk.

【Day 3】
Wednesday

MP3 011

Question 05

My mother gets running nose because she stays in air-condition rooms for too long.

I usually sneeze and my respiratory system becomes uncomfortable when seasons change.

My father's skin rashes when he eats seafood and milk.

Question 06

MP3 012

Air pollution and weather cause my allergic reactions.

Temperature and moist change are my mother's allergen.

Allergens from particular foods bring my father some allergic reactions.

MP3 013

Questions 7–9: Respond to questions using information provided

Directions: In this part of the test, you will answer three questions based on the information provided. You will have 30 seconds to read the information before the questions begin. For each question, begin responding immediately after you hear a beep. No additional preparation time is provided. You will have 15 seconds to respond to Questions 7 and 8, and 30 seconds to respond to Question 9.

The Asia-Pacific Conference on Political Sciences

Date: Feb. 20th~ Mar. 21th, 2014

Location: Hong Kong

The Asia-Pacific Conference on Social Science 2014 is one of the leading international conferences to present novel and fundamental advances in the fields of Political Science. It also serves to foster communication among researchers and practitioners working in a wide variety of scientific areas with a common interest in improving Political Science.

Keynote Speech:

"Influences of New Media And Technology On Cultural and Political Change"

Prof. John Tennyson, the author ofInfluences of New Media And Technology On Cultural and Political Change.

Book signing: 11: 00 A.M. Feb. 20th, Grand meeting Room.

MP3 014

Listen to question 7:

This is Angela Norton. I am planning to attend the The Asia-Pacific Conference on Political Sciences, but I lost the original invitation, so I need some information.

MP3 015

Listen to the question 8:

I don't know who is Professor John Tennyson. Can you help me?

MP3 016

Listen to the question 9:

Besides the lecture from the main speaker, what else is going on?

Answers to:

MP3 017

7. The conference will be held from February20th to March 21st, 2014 in Hong Kong. Professor John Tennyson will deliver the keynote Speech.

MP3 018

8. He is the author of Influences of New Media And Technology On Cultural and Political Change.

MP3 019

9. There will be a book signing at 11: 00 A.M., February 20th in the Grand meeting Room.

MP3 020

Question 1: Describe your father. (15seconds)(beep sound)

Question 2: Are you an organized person? Why or why not? (15seconds)(beep sound)

Question 3: You're watching a movie in a theater. Suddenly, the fire alarm goes off. What will you do next? (15seconds)(beep sound)

Question 4: Why are there more and more problems of food security? (15seconds)(beep sound)

Question 5: What are two things we should pay attention to when we drive? Why? (15seconds)(beep sound)

Question 6: Do you go hiking a lot? If so, tell me about your experience. If not, tell me something you know about hiking. (30seconds) (beep sound)

Question 7: Tell me one of your hobbies? Why do you like it? (30seconds) (beep sound)

Question 8: What kinds of foods should you eat to be healthy? Why? (30seconds) (beep sound)

Question 9: Why is it important to reduce energy use? (30seconds) (beep sound)

Question 10: Describe your favorite free time activity. How was it last time? (30seconds) (beep sound)

Answers to Question no. 1

MP3 021

My father is an English teacher. He is a little strict but a good father. He is very patient with us just as he is with his students. He gave us the goals of life with simple but firm instructions.

MP3 022

My father is a military man. He is unbending in setbacks and humble and gentle when he gets ahead. He always tells us that knowing ourselves is the foundation of knowledge.

Answers to Question 2

MP3 023

Yes, I'm an organized person. I keep my room tidy, my bed clean, and never forget doing the laundry. I've never been late to school and I turn in my assignments on time.

【Day 5】
Friday

MP3 024

No, I'm not an organized person. My room is always messy with dirty underwear, smelly socks, and scattered books. What's worse, I can't catch up with schedules, and my works are often overdue.

Answers to Question 3
MP3 025

Actually, I don't know what to do then. Since the panic crowd may be in my way, I will rush the faster the better. If the smoke gets dense, I guess all I could do is to stay low and crawl to the nearest exit.

MP3 026

If the alarm goes off, I will inform the people around me there is a fire. Next, I will tell people to follow the emergency instruction, and then assist individuals with disabilities and others if it is safe to do so.

Answers to Question 4
MP3 027

I think government agencies fail to protect their citizens from consuming tainted oil. Food companies are the ones to be blamed. After all, they buy that oil, knowing that the source is from the recycled waste oil. What's worse, they sold it to loyal customers. maintain foremost control in protecting our food supply. That's why the food company was able to buy recycled waste oil and mix it with lard oil to resell to customers.

MP3 028

I think the tainted oil is the main cause of our food safety problems. Tons of popular products, including seasonal mooncakes, pineapple cakes, breads, instant noodles, steamed buns, and dumplings have been contaminated.

Answers to Question 5:

MP3 029

I think talking and texting are the two main driver distractions on the driver's list. Using a cellphone while driving is illegal, let alone texting messages.

【Day 5】
Friday

MP3 030

I think daydreaming while driving is also very dangerous, and it's one of the most serious problems on the driving list. The problem will be aggravated by fatigue and a wandering mind. We should sleep well before driving and focus on the road right in front of us.

Answers to Question 6
MP3 031

I like hiking. It's a healthy way to spend wonderful time with friends. Hiking is a good way to get some exercise. It's a mixture of excellent aerobic activities and life enjoyment. The experience of hiking is unimaginable. It has created an unforgettable memory in your life. Hiking doesn't necessarily have to take high risk and difficult challenge. Hiking can be done in any wooded area or even a local public park.

MP3 032

Although I'm not familiar with hiking, I know gear is the necessity. Hiking can be a pleasant activity if everyone is outfitted in the appropriate gear. For example, comfortable sneakers or hiking boots, a backpack big enough, light enough to carry all of the snacks and other things needed on the trail. Make sure that you have a good camera so that you can record memories along the way.

Answers to Question no. 7:
MP3 033

Writing software is my hobby. During my years at college, I helped create a website to solve all homework problems. Even today, some of my classmates are my big fans of the website. Since then the software has now been a part of people's life.

MP3 034

My hobbies are mostly restricted to outdoor activities. Among all hobbies, fishing is my favorite. I like to have fishing trips with friends. I started fishing at the age of 13, and now I run a fishing club with hundreds of members. The hobby not only gives me a great pleasure but a good career life. However, I am also an environmentalist; I do go fishing for fun, but will never damage the ecological balance.

Answers to Question 8:

MP3 035

Acid Fruits such as lemons,oranges, grapefruits, peaches, limes, tangerines, grapes, tomatoes, pineapples, apples, are excellent foods with the most detoxifying ingredients. Some people may have problems with these fruits because of their acid content. The acid though is a healthy and organic nutritional element; for instance, ascorbic acid is vitamin C, found especially in citrus fruits and vegetables.

MP3 036

Rye bread and flaxseed bread are the healthiest types of bread that you can eat daily without worrying about calories. They are fantastic bread for weight loss and it's an excellent source of mineral ingredients. Flaxseed bread also contains essential fatty acids and dietary fiber that will help boost your

【Day 5】
Friday

health and get your dream body shape. Rye bread is absolutely wheat-free, and it can help relieve discomfort and bloating.

Answers to Question 9:
MP3 037

While we need Energy to power our cars, cook our food, light up our homes, and so much more, many of us become wasteful and actually use much more that we actually need. This excess can cause unnecessary, avoidable pollution. Pollution harms the air quality that we inhale outside. It also negatively impacts wildlife such as plants, trees, and animals.

MP3 038

Energy savings can help us from a financial standpoint. Since energy is in higher and higher demand, prices continue to rise, costing householders a fortune. When you reduce your energy use, you are able to cut down on your energy bills, so more money can be saved from your pocket! Our hard earned money shouldn't be wasted on energy in places of things we truly want.

Answers to Question 10:
MP3 039

My favorite free time activity is hiking. Last time I hiked Ali Mountain, which is worldwide famous for its "five rare sites" including the Sunrise, the Ali Mountain Forest Railway, the famous Alishan Sacred Tree, the Grand Sea of Clouds, and the Flamboyant Cherry Blossom. I would never know its wonderful beauty before paying a visit there.

MP3 040

My favorite free time activity is fishing. Last time, I went fishing at Sun moon Lake. The weather was beautiful that day. I consulted with a local guide to get the actual sunrise and sunset plus moon rise and moon set timetable. My fishing trip was successful and I caught a full bag of Tilapia. They are fun to catch.

【Day 5】
Friday

MP3 041

Part 3

Directions: In this section of the test, you will hear a number of conversations between two people. You will be asked to answer three questions about what is said in each conversation. You must select the best response to each question and mark the letter (A), (B), (C), or (D)on your answer sheet. Each conversation will be spoken only one time and will not be printed in your test book.

Questions 1 and 2 refer to the following conversation.

    Man: Anything important in that report?

  Woman: Well, three inmates fled last night. They also stole 3 guns.

    Man: How did the inmates get out?

  Woman: They made a tunnel under the floor and crawled out of the prison. But how they stole the guns is not yet known. Maybe they stole them at some other time.

1. What is true about the report?

2. What will the inmates probably do next?

MP3 042

Questions 3 through 5 refer to the following conversation.

Man 1: Hello, Mr. James. My name's Tony. I'd like to buy a mobile phone, but I know nothing about them. Can you help?

Man 2: It'd be better if you could come and see me and we'll find the right mobile phone for you.

Man 1: Oh! Great! I'll go tomorrow. I'll take the subway at 10 o'clock. I think I have to change at Central Park, but it is a short wait and I will arrive at 5th Avenue before 11 o'clock. Can you tell me how far it is from the station to your shop?

3. What will happen tomorrow morning?

4. When might be the time that they see each other?

5. What will Mr. James do next?

MP3 043

Questions 6 through 8 refer to the following conversation.

Man: It was a nice car. I thought you had a great time driving.

Woman: I used to, but I sold it. It was a four-wheel drive vehicle, consuming too much fuel for me. Besides, I have already had a smaller car. It's a more economical one.

Man: That sounds great. Can I see it sometime?

Woman: Of course. It's in the garage if you'd like to see it now.

6. Why did the woman sell the car?

7. Where does this conversation take place?

8. What will happen next?

MP3 044

Questions 9 and 10 refer to the following conversation.

Man: I had a wonderful night yesterday. While I was worried about losing my job, the other company called me and offered a better position. When I checked my account, I found a generous payment in advance!

Woman: Did you call your wife right away?

Man: Yes, and she said I would never let her down.

Woman: Well, I bet you are!

9. What happened to the man last night?

10. What is the man probably "NOT" going to do next?

MP3 045

Questions 11 and 12 refer to the following conversation.

Woman: Dad, I want to take part in the marathon inChina with Yvonne and Sonia.

Man: I'm not sure, Denise. Who is coaching you?

Woman: Mr. Louis, you know him. We've practiced for months and we are all in good shape. Everything for the race is ready. We would go for ten days to two weeks.

Man: I'll talk to your mother this evening. But I'm not making any promises.

11. What will happen if Denise goes on the trip?

12. Why didn't Denise's father just say "Yes"?

MP3 046

(Extended conversation)

(1-2)

Man: What do you think the inmates will probably do next?

Woman: Of course, they should find the inmates as soon as possible!

Man: What if they can't find them? These fugitives are walking time bombs with deadly weapons.

Woman: I guess the law enforcement agencies are going to have a hard time.

MP3 047

(3-5)

Man 1: Hello, Mr. James. It's Tony, and I have arrived at 5th Avenue right now at 11 o'clock, but I really got lost around the block here. Could you tell me how to find your shop?

Man 2: Try to find the cross road sign for East 36th Street and 5th Avenue. There is a tall building with the Stars and Stripes on the pillars. Just wait there at the corner, and I'll personally pick you up.

Man 1: Thanks a lot!

MP3 048

（6-8）

Man: This car is brand new. Why do you want to sell it?

Woman: Well, I'm moving to another country. Everything you see around is about to be auctioned later.

Man: Why didn't you say so? You could have put this car together with others in an ad of auction.

Woman: Because I know you are a car lover. The car deserves a better owner.

MP3 049

（9-10）

Man: I can't wait to see the look of my boss when I tell him that I'm going to leave.

Woman: I don't think that will make him surprised. After all, you are to leave whether you quit or not.

MP3 050

（11-12）

Woman: Why don't you just say "Yes," Dad? It's your idea asking me to play more sports, and Mom also said she would wholeheartedly endorse it.

Man: Yes, that's what I said, but I didn't expect that China is your concern. It's such a long journey of some places you have never been before, and how do I know that you will be taken care of as it is due?

Woman: Daddy, I'm a big girl now. I know what I'm doing!

Man: Just let me ask your mother's opinion, and see if she still agrees to it now.

MP3 051

Directions: In this section of the test, you will hear a number of conversations between two people. You will be asked to answer three questions about what is said in each conversation. You must select the best response to each question and mark the letter (A), (B), (C), or (D) on your answer sheet. Each conversation will be spoken only one time and will not be printed in your test book.

31. W: Tom, are you going abroad tomorrow?

　　M: Yes, why?

　　W: Could you bring me a bottle of perfume from the duty free store when you come back? I need one of Chanel.

　　M: Sure, no problem.

　　Q: Why did the woman talk to the man?

32. M: Can I see your paper, please?

　　W: I wasn't cheating, was I?

　　M: That's what I'm trying to find out.

　　W: I do all the answers by myself. Look, here they are.

　　M: Then, you should put them only on your sheet, not on your legs.

　　W: They are just tattoos. Please, don't take my paper away, sir.

M：Sorry.

Q：Who is the man?

33. W：Can I help you?

M：Yes, I'd like two bags of flour, a dozen eggs, and a bottle of milk.

W：Two bags of flour, a dozen eggs, and a bottle of milk. Low fat or full cream?

M：Low fat, please.

W：And by credit card or in cash?

M：Credit card. Here you are.

W：O.K. That's $155. Have a nice day.

Q：Where did this conversation take place?

34. M：Judy, I think you might be excited by this commercial. Cosmetics are on sale at Sincere.

W：Sincere? Oh, is that near the MRT station at First Avenue?

M：Yes, that's the one. Here's the web site.

W：Thanks. I'll be ready to purchase a lot.

Q：What are the speakers talking about?

35. W：Did you watch "Art and Your Life" on A Max last night?

M：Yes, I did. How do you think about the program?

W：I like the part about Vincent.

M：Vincent? What's that about?

W：I was impressed by his flaming flowers of bright blaze and swirling clouds in violet haze that reflect in Vincent's eyes of china blue.

Q：Where did the woman learn about "Vincent"?

36. W：Mark, what happened? The meeting has started for 30 minutes. Did you miss the train again?

M：I'm sorry, Jen. My car broke down on the way.

W：Since when did you start driving?

Q：Why is Mark late?

37. W：OK, now. We are supposed to leave now. John, pack your bags up!

M：Why don't we stay for one more night? It's still early to go home.

W：Yeah, but we are over the budget. We'd better check out before they ask us to.

Q：Why do they have to check out?

38. M：Excuse me, could you tell me how to get to Taipei 101?

W：Let me see... oh, yeah, you can take the MRT and get off at the Taipei City Hall station. Then walk for a few blocks. You will see the huge building.

M：MRT and get off at the Taipei City hall station. OK, I got it. Thanks a lot.

W：You're welcome.

Q：According to the woman, how can the man get to Taipei 101?

39. M：What's wrong, Anny? You look frightened.

　W：I've just seen a horrible car accident! All the passengers were seriously injured.

　M：Well, why don't you call the police first?

　W：Because the victims have been the policemen!

　Q：What does Anny mean?

40. M：Don't forget our flight tomorrow morning.

　W：At 8, right?

　M：Yes. But we have to be there an hour early to check in.

.　W：We shouldn't have any problem. Everything we need for the trip has been packed up.

　M：Not including the souvenir we ordered from this hotel.

　W：Oh, I almost forgot that. When is the arrival?

　Q：What does the man mean?

41. W：Hello, is Cindy there?

　M：No, she's not at her table now. Maybe she will be back in a minute. Do you want to leave a message?

　W：Yes. This is Maggie. Cindy and I are going to a party tonight. Would you please remind her it's a Halloween night? Tell her to remember the make-up.

M：All right, Maggie. I'll remind her.

Q：What message did Maggie leave?

42. M：I heard you are admitted to New York University.
   Congratulations!

   W：Thanks. Yes, I'm ready for the Broadway, Times Square,
   Seventh Avenue, and all the fancy shows there.

   M：Excuse me—aren't you supposed to get your degree
   in two years? How could you make it with all these
   hangouts?

   W：Oh, don't you remember my project is exactly about
   show business?

   Q：　　What is the woman ready to study?

43. M：I heard John is applying for a journalism program. He
   must be dreaming of winning the Pulitzer Prize.

   W：Well, he's always had an ambition of being a press
   magnate. Remember that he once made a great report for
   the local newspaper?

   M：Yeah! Think about if he made it to run his own newspaper
   someday!

   Q：What do the two speakers think about John?

44. W：Jason, can you sort these books out for me?

　　M：Of course, Mendy. How are you going to classify them? I don't know much about librarianship.

　　W：Oh, that's my job. All you have to do is to stack them by different returned dates.

　　M：Maybe we can arrange some shelves with returning dates for people to return books.

　　W：That's a good idea. I'll put some shelves in the hall later.

　　Q：What will Mendy and Jason probably do next?

45. M：I just saw an amazing job in the newspaper.

　　W：Oh yeah? What does it say?

　　M：Well, the salary is far higher than my previous position, and they offer a car for transportation.

　　W：Sounds good. Where is it located?

　　M：Downtown, near your office.

　　W：Wow. That sounds too good to be true. How much is the salary?

　　M：It's $80,000 a month.

　　W：$80,000 a month! That's twice mine! Watch out for fraud!

　　Q：What does the woman think about the job?

MP3 052

Listen to the following conversation

Extended conversation

35. M: You just recited Don McLean's song "Vincent -Starry, Starry Night."

    W: You're right. The Starry Night is an oil painting on canvas. It depicts the view of an idealized village.

    M: Well, I am more concerned about Don McLean's song. He challenged the idea of turning the picture into music.

    W: I know that, and in 1972the songVincent reached number 1 hit in the UK and number 12 in the USA.

36. M: I forgot to tell you that I bought a car last week and I hardly use it myself until today.

    W: How coincident is that the car broke down the first time you drove it?

    M: Well, it just happened.

    W: OK! We are looking forward to seeing your new car.

37. M: How could we be over the budget? Didn't we set all the budgets before this trip?

    W: Right, but I just bought some jewelry in the lobby shop

that cost all the rest of the money we had, and we can't afford to spend one more night.

M：Alright my dear. You may well do that as it is our honey moon, as long as you think it is worthy!

38. M：So, are you taking the MRT too?

W：Yes, and I happened to get off at the Taipei City Hall station.

M：Oh, really? Do you mind me in company with you on this trip?

W：No, and would you tell me why you're going to Taipei 101?

M：Of course, I am on a tour visiting the highest view of the world.

39. M：Did you see how the accident happened?

W：Yes. That's why I'm scared to death.

M：Don't be nervous. You'll do fine. What exactly did you see?

W：There were police cars pursuing others cars of outlaws, and they were shooting each other until the police car was wrecked.

M：Wow! That must be a thrilling scene to you and it sounds so exciting. It's like in a movie.

W：Don't play with me. I haven't got over it yet.

40. M : I don't know. You didn't tell me. Why don't you ask the lobby shop?

  W1 : You're right. I'll call them now. (Dial the phone) Hello, this is Mrs. Tomson speaking from room 1203. Can you tell me when my ordered item will arrive? I ordered it yesterday.

  W2 : One moment please. Ah, It has been here for a while, we'll deliver it to your room immediately.

  W1 : Thank you.

MP3 053

Extended Conversation

41. M : Cindy, Maggie just called to remind you of the party tonight. She wanted to remind you the Halloween's make-up.

  W : I know. I just went shopping, buying some pirate costumes for the party.

  M : Oh, is that old scroll stained with coffee in a bottle your invitation? That's awesome!

  W : Yeah, that's her pirate-themed party except too spooky this year.

  M : Why? You can wear any spooky costume you want without a care in the world! Isn't it?

W: Right, but playing a disgusting zombie pirate is my last option.

42. M: I remember, but I thought it was the same as any other courses in the class rooms.

W: Not exactly, I learn that the entertainment industry is a field ranging from managers to artists. You can't just sit in an armchair to learn this industry.

M: I see. You need an actual field observation to evaluate your theories.

W: You're right this time.

43. W: According to his dream, he will have to be a successful entrepreneur or businessperson to deal with problems in such fields as television networks, film studios, publishing houses, and internet or multimedia companies rather than newspaper.

M: That requires more skills than news reporting. It doesn't seem practical for him with his sole talent as a journalist.

W: Maybe, but where there is a will, there is a way.

44. M: Are you a collection development librarian?

W: Yes I am.

M: What do you actually do?

W: I monitor the selection of books and electronic resources

【Day 4】
Thursday

and create profiles that allow publishers to send relevant books to the library. Then I can see those books when they arrive and decide if they will become a part of the collection or not.

45. M : I heard some cases of employment fraud. Is that what you mean?

W : Exactly, it's an attempt to defraud people who are seeking better jobs by giving them a false hope of the better position with higher wages just like your case might be.

M : Are there promises such as easy work, high wages for unskilled labor, and flexible hours?

W : Now you got the picture.

MP3 054

M : We don't have enough facilities for fun at the science park. Why can't we have more art galleries, play grounds, and dancing halls?

W : You're right. But do you know about the new employee activity fee?

M : No. What's it about?

W : Well, it means more budgets for things like that.

M : You're saying that our painting club will really get any of the budget, aren't you?

W : Well, it could.

M : How?

W : Well, I checked out the company web site. They're giving $800 to each registered employee organization. So, if it's not already, we should get our painting club registered. Then, we can ask for $3,800 more after that with another special program!

M : Wow! What are we waiting for? What exactly is the web site?

W : It's the Apple Activities Park. In fact, they're looking for employee organizations right now.

M : Really! How do they have so much money?

W : Well, every new employee at our company pays $20 into

the fund. It started this month. That wouldn't be too much money for the coming years, so our CEO put in more money. It comes from other programs at the company.

M: Oh, I see. So we can do some exhibitions for our painting club! Remember that we were thinking of the expressionist art display?

W: Yes, of course! That's why I was checking on the website!

(Extended conversation)

MP3 055

M: You know? We have a problem of collecting membership fee. Were you able to find the solution?

W: We were successful when we started the painting club until we failed to display their works to the public. I think now we have some steps of the solution after we found the funds for the club. First, members need to realize they need a stage after all. Many of them found that they got less, even no chances to display their works after they left the club. It takes time to find a stage, and now it's easy to expect. Second, we need more fun parties for our members, so they can share their experiences of creativity. By doing so, they could find even more satisfaction than displaying art works in a cold gallery. Then, they wouldn't complain about missing a stage because they could have already been on a stage.

M : Wow, it sounds like a great plan of yours. Are you sure they will be as eager for a party as for a gallery?

W : We should be more aggressive promoting our new ideas. We talk with them about the new plan and see how they think. People with a strong passion for painting will express their opinions.

M : So when do we start to carry on?

W : After we get the money.

WEEK **3** 簡短談話篇錄音稿

DAY 1 MONDAY

Part C

In part C, you will hear several short talks. After each talk, you will hear 2 to 3 questions about the talk. After you hear each question, read the four choices in your test book and choose the best answer to the question you have heard.

[Questions number 1 and 2 are based on the following story.]

Ms. Mary Delson is an Afro-American woman living in New Jersey. She has been working as a waitress for over 60 years. The day when she retired, she surprisingly found that her monthly pittance had made over $100,000 in savings. Then the even greater surprise for people, she gave away most of her savings to a charity fund for African-American students. The press highlighted her kindness.

Question number 1: What did Ms. Mary Delson do to make her famous?

Question number 2: What did the reporter say about Ms. Mary Delson?

[Questions number 3 to 5 are based on the following talk.]

Hello, Mr. Brown, the message is from Dr. Johnson. I had my assistant call you back yesterday, but I haven't heard your reply since then. Now I'm personally giving you the message today, because you may have excellent good news about what you are concerned about. The point is that the hospital is going to budget $ one million for your surgical table. It appears to be good for operations in the areas of the chest, abdomen, gynaecology, obstetrics, and orthopaedics. You've been promoting this project for more than one year. It's now paid off, congratulations! We are expecting your further presentation about the new equipment. Please contact us soon!

Question number 3: Who is the speaker talking to?

Question number 4: What is the speaker mainly talking about?

Question number 5: What does the speaker want the listener to do now?

[Questions number 6 and 7 are based on the following news report.]

Good morning! It's the seven o'clock news report from TNN. For those parents who are listening to our program, "How do your children go to school now?" Do they ride a motorcycle? The big questions are, are they texting while riding, and are you texting while driving? Today's news includes the statistics on the risk of driving and texting. You're 23 times more likely to crash while texting and driving, let alone texting and riding. You may think it is incredible to text messages while riding, but it just happened 2 hours ago: two teenagers texted each other while riding a motor cycle before they both crashed and are in critical condition.

Question number 6: What is the speaker's purpose?

Question number 7: What aspect of texting does the speaker emphasize?

[Questions number 8 and 9 are based on the following talk in a dormitory tour.]

OK, students. Let's begin today's dormitory tour with the facilities. As we are here, this is the lobby with a TV set and a magazine shelf. Please do not bring the magazines to your room or rest your shoes on the couch and coffee table. If you need to do laundry, we have four coin-operated washing machines and dryers down the hallway. We also have a recreation room next to the lobby with two ping pong tables. The most important thing when living here is to check in through the sensor gate with your student card. You can't get in without matching your fingerprint and the card on the scanner. Please follow me and I'll show you how it works.

Question number 8: Where should a person go if he needs to do laundry?

Question number 9: What is the speaker going to do now?

[Questions number 10 to 12 are based on the following announcement.]

Shoppers, may I have your attention, please? We're having a happy mother's day sale this week. Over 1,000 items are marked down to just 10 dollars each. There are various pans, irons, kettles, toothbrushes, pastes, and jars at this price. If you're a VIP card holder, you can enjoy a further 15% discount. These sales are amazing, aren't they? You don't want to miss out on this great opportunity, do you? These great deals won't last long. There are three more days left. Grab what you need while you can. Happy shopping!

Question number 10: How much longer will the sale last?

Question number 11: What is the price of each marked down item?

Question number 12: What benefit can VIP card holders enjoy?

[Questions number 13 to 15 are based on the following movie review.]

The Stranger is one of the best movies I've ever seen. It's based on the famous book The Lonely Woman In the Village by Martha Roberts. The movie starts with the divorce of a woman in a village followed by a cheating man who is having an affair with a girl next door. As the story proceeds, all the man and girl's families move away from the village. As a result, only the divorced woman and the man were left as neighbors. One day, the man shows up in her front yard. Will she change her mind to accept him? Or does the man mean to come back? The ending is quite surprising. Julia Lopez, who plays the woman in this movie, is excellent in the role. Certainly, the movie would not be successful without William Smith, the leading actor. He is in line to win the best actor award because of this movie. Overall, it is definitely going to be one of the hits this summer. Don't miss it.

Question number 13: What is the purpose of this review?

Question number 14: Who shows up in the woman's front yard?

Question number 15: What will the leading actor probably win because of this movie?

Expanded talks
MP3 057

1.

When Ms. Mary Delson was interviewed by the press, she was extremely humble. As an Afro-American woman living in New Jersey, her only dream was to take Afro-American history at university, but at her age then, she said, her dream would come true by helping young black generations with their education. She saw a need to develop an appreciation for the historic and cultural heritage of African Americans. Just about the same time she retired with a decent sum of money, she learned the Afro-American Historical Society Museum was in need of donations for further development of the historical and cultural African American exhibitions and programs for scholarships. "What a coincidence to me and this solicitation," she said, "and what am I waiting for?"

MP3 058

2.

Hello, Mr. Brown, the message is from Dr. Johnson. I had my assistant call you back yesterday, but I haven't heard your reply since then. Now I'm personally giving you the message because we do have excellent news for you. The point is that the hospital is going to budget $ one million for your surgical table. It appears to be good for operations in the areas of the chest, abdomen, gynaecology, obstetrics, and orthopaedics. You've been promoting this project for more than a year. It's now paid off, congratulations! We are expecting your further presentation about the new equipment. Please contact us soon!

MP3 059

3.

Hello Dr. Johnson, this is Mr. Brown calling as requested. I'm excited to hear the news. Since you are anxious to learn how the surgical operation table works, I'll now give you a preliminary briefing. It is a device including first, a master that detects the movement of the body of an operator and second, a slave that performs surgery on the tissue by movement of the operator. The information is supplied from the master, and the slave holds a surgical appliance on an area. This is what I'm going to present in your board meeting. Call me if there are any other questions.

Expanded talks

MP3 060

1.

In this accident, there was a collision with two motorcycles. The witness said the riders of the motorcycles were texting and not paying attention to the road, and as a result they crashed into the gutter by the road. With that the motorcycles were completely smashed in the front and almost completely twisted. The motorcycles were in pieces. The names of these two persons are still unknown, and the policemen are trying to identify them with their mutilated bodies. These riders were stupid because they were texting while riding. Their lives ended because of the stupid mistake they made, even if they had done it many times before.

MP3 061

2.

For the new registered students, go to the Office of Student Residence website for "the password to the dormitory gate." For those who have applied for a password, here are the following tips: first, enter your student ID number and the last four digits of your birthday, and then press your fingers on the censor for the prints. Second, to enter the dormitory, enter the password you applied into the door card reader by the gate. Last but not the least, the password can only be used for the dormitory the student is residing in.

MP3 062

3.

Don't you love a good shopping trip on Mother's Day? We're enjoying all the Disney's shows at happy mother's day website, so we're celebrating with a sale! Give your Disney's baby wearing a boost with a new wrap, just in time for Mother's Day! Take $60 off wrap orders of $120 or more and $120 off

$225 or more! Which wraps have you had your eyes on? Hurry up, or the wait is over! Remember, this sale only qualifies for the new woven and stretchy wraps. This sale will run through Sunday, but for the best selection, shop quickly!

MP3 063

4

The most important interpersonal communication principles exemplify in this movie The Stranger are: First, intercultural communication: the girl's family next door is from a different race. Therefore, her interactions not only with her neighborhood but others in public or school are not friendly. When they move to the village for the first time, other neighbors avoid them. Second, self-concept: the girl meets criticism from her friends as to what she is doing with a white man next door she actually calls him sir. She needs a white family to balance her awkward identity, which is exactly made up by the white man with a sense of authority. The man, however, is in a confusion of tiresome marriage, bumps into this accidental sparks of affection out of another confusion between admiration and safety.

MP3 064

[Questions number 1to 3 are based on the following talk.]

Now, we are going to show you how to apply for the school. You should apply for this status if you have never attended a college or a university before. First, you must earn a diploma from an accredited high school before enrolling at this school. Make sure to check our admission standards and deadlines before you start the application process. Second, all applicants should use the same application form to apply for the school, entering any programs on our campus. Last, after you submit your application and all of your materials, you will usually wait for three to five weeks if you have been admitted. Learn more about what happens after you apply, including how to check your admission status.

Question number 1: What is the speaker doing?
Question number 2: Who is most probably listening to the talk?
Question number 3: What is the first thing the listener has to do?

[Questions number 4 and 5 are based on the following announcement.]

Hello. Passengers of flight FA112 are heading for Paris, with stops in Rio De Janeiro. It's two thirty pm local time. The departure gate has changed to 40B. Also, there will be a slight departure delay due to severe weather outside. The ground crew is in the process of deicing the wings in preparation for departure. It also looks like the flight is slightly overbooked, so we are offering complimentary round-trip tickets to a few passengers willing to take a later flight. We should be boarding about a quarter to three. Thank you for your patience.

Question number 4: When should the passengers board now?
Question number 5: What caused the problem?

[Questions number 6 and 7 are based on the following news report.]

Welcome to the evening report. Today is Friday, a necessary getting drunk evening, but are you driving now? Driving under the influence incidents have fallen 40 percent in the past six years, and last year it was at their lowest mark in nearly three decades, according to the latest national report. The decrease may be due to the economy downturn: Other research suggests people are still drinking as heavily as they were in years past, so some may just be looking for cheaper ways of imbibing than by going to bars, night clubs, and restaurants. "One possibility is that more people are drinking at home more and fewer people are driving after drinking," said Dr. Theodore Frank, director of the Institute of Accident Control and Prevention.

Question number 6: What is the speaker's purpose?

Question number 7: What aspect of driving under the influence does the speaker emphasize?

[Questions number 8 and 9 are based on the following talk.]

Hello, shoppers. Do you think it is troublesome to make coffee when you are at home? Do you buy coffee in stores for its convenience? Well, here's a machine that will totally save you money. It's called the Extrapresso coffeemaker. It is capable of making striking, consistent, normal and strong coffee. Let me show you how it works. First, Grasp the filter cup and pull it straight out. Insert a standard coffee filter into the cup. Scoop one to two tablespoons of ground coffee per cup of coffee that you want to brew. Insert the filter cup back into its mount. Remove the glass carafe from the plate. Then fill it with water. Use the markings on the side as a guide. Add an amount of water in line with the amount of coffee you added. Last, re-insert the glass carafe onto the plate. Plug the machine in and press the "On" switch located on the side. The Extrapresso begins heating the water and brewing the coffee. Buy this Extrapresso coffeemaker and start saving money on coffee today!

Question number 8: Where is this talk most probably being given?

Question number 9: What is a special feature of the Extrapresso coffeemaker?

【Day 3】
Wednesday

[Questions number 10 to 12 are based on the following narration.]

Hayao Miyazaki is the great anime director of fantastic films like Spirited Away and Howl's Moving Castle. He is always serious about making good anime, often working extra as a writer for the anime he directs.

Born in 1941, Miyazaki loved drawing airplanes as a boy. After he saw a first ever colored animation when he was in high school, his interest in anime grew and he started drawing people as well. Influenced by his mother, who loved questioning common ideas, he creates characters that have surprising and unique qualities. In 1997, the film Princess Mononoke made him really famous. It achieved great popularity in Japan, and it was his first film that made its way to the West. Afterwards, he made Spirited Away, which broke box office records in 2001 and received many awards, including an Oscar for Best Animated Feature.

Question number 10: What is the main focus of this talk?

Question number 11: When did Hayao Miyazaki become really famous?

Question number 12: Which film of Hayao Miyazaki's broke the box office record?

[Questions number 13 to 15 are based on the following talk.]

All right, to wrap up, because different animals use their digestive systems in different ways, a variety of digestive systems are required in the animal kingdom. The following are different examples. One, sloths: with slow-moving nature, his digestive system can take up to a month to process his food. Two, cows: A cow's stomach is divided into four sections. The first section softens the cow's food. The second section sends the food back up to the mouth where it can be rechewed. The third section removes the moisture from food and the last section is the mixture of food and digestive juices. Third, dogs: dog's intestinal tract is shorter than a human's, due to the amount of protein dogs consume. Fourth, whales: they have a three-sectioned stomach. The first section of a whale's stomach breaks down its food by crushing. The second section mixes the food with digestive juices and the third further mixes the food and digestive juices. Fifth, birds, its two-chambered stomach mixes the food with digestive acids and crushes the food thoroughly.

Question number 13: When was the talk most probably given?

Question number 14: How many examples did the speaker just mention?

Question number 15: What does the speaker say about the digestive system of dogs?

Expanded talks

MP3 065

1.

Welcome! Our school offers all catagories of highly ranked academic and professional degree programs, and we encourage talented students either throughout the United States or from abroad to apply. The school is seeking students who can benefit from a wealth of academic and cultural opportunities. The committee offers the admission to applicants who have the highest potential to succeed in the graduate study and who are more likely to have a substantial impact on their chosen field. We value our graduate students as important participants in the scholarship and research conducted at this school.

MP3 066

2.

Ladies and gentlemen, welcome on board Flight FA112 with service from San Francisco to Paris. The flight scheduled for 2:45 was delayed till 3 pm, but now rescheduled to 4 pm. We are sorry for your inconvenience. We are expected to take off in approximately seven minutes. Please fasten your seatbelts at this time and secure all baggage beneath your seat or in the overhead compartments. We also ask that your seats and table trays are in the upright position for take-off. Please turn off all personal electronic devices, including laptops and cell phones.

Smoking is prohibited for the duration of the flight. Thank you for choosing USS Airlines. Enjoy your flight.

Expanded talks

MP3 067

1.

Now let's look at the latest report, a New York mother was responsible for a deadly car accident that killed herself and four children in her car, and three men traveling in another vehicle. When the toxicology reports came out, the mother's blood alcohol level was 0.2 percent, nearly twice the legal limit for drivers.

The national studies show that the abuse of alcohol has been increasing among women. Moreover, while driving under the influence of alcohol arrests have decreased over the past ten years for men. It has increased in women. In fact, the government statistics show that driving under the influence arrests among women was increased by almost 30% in women when comparing 1998 with 2008.

【Day 4】
Thursday

MP3 068

2.

OK, follow me and I'll show you how to operate the photo copy machine.

First, inspect the original documents. Remove staples, paper clips or binder clips holding pages together. Smooth wrinkled or folded pages excessively.

Second, insert the original documents face up into the automatic document feeder. The feeder mounts directly over the plate glass or just to the side on the top of the copier. Third, press the number keys to select the number of copies you want. Fourth, Press the "Start" button on the control panel or the "Start" soft key on the touch display to begin the copy process. Last, remove the copies from the output tray after the copy process has finished. Remove your originals from the automatic document feeder.

MP3 069

3.

Claude Monet is a famous French artist as well as one of the founders of the Impressionism art movement of the 1870s and 1880s. The art movement got its name from one of Monet's paintings, Impression, Sunrise. Monet was inspired by the Realists in his early twenties. He loves nature and loves to paint in the fresh air. But rather than depicting the real world in a naturalistic way, Monet observed variations of color and light caused by the daily or seasonal changes. For each person, there is no unchanging landscape that exists independently of our perceptions. We can only perceive the important thing, which would change from moment to moment as the air and light continually changing the surroundings and atmosphere. He thought it was these changing conditions that influenced the subjects of the art with their only true value.

MP3 070

4.

There are a variety of petroleum alternatives available for cars. They were developed because of soaring gas and diesel prices. A handful are being explored and aren't as widely available on today's market. For example, ethanol is a fuel made from plant materials, often wheat or corn. As such, it is a renewable fuel source for cars and is considered an option for environmentally friendly vehicles. Others like biodiesel are typically made from vegetable oils like corn and canola. These are usually considered a renewable resource because they are made from plants. They are also two of the leading fuel alternatives considered by environmentalists.

【Day 4】
Thursday

MP3 071

Questions 1 and 2 refer to the following talk.

Jim Brown likes his job. He is an engineer. He and his wife live in New York but they are from Canada. They have a big apartment near a park. They have three children. Their names are Tony, Jane, and Monica. Mary Brown is a teacher. She works in New York, too. She has a car and drives to work. The car was made in Germany. Jim doesn't have a car, but he has a motorcycle. He rides the motorcycle to work in New Jersey.

1. What is the talk mainly about?
   (A) Life in the United States
   (B) The Brown family
   (C) A Family Reunion
   (D) Some Big Cities in the world

2. Which of the following statements about Jim is true?
   (A) He is from Germany.
   (B) He has no sons.
   (C) Jim works in New Jersey.
   (D) He lives in Canada.

Questions 3 to 5 refer to the following talk.

Adam flew to China. His plane was scheduled to leave at 10 a.m. Adam made it in two hours to reach the airport and to check in. He arrived at the airport at 9 a.m. He checked in his luggage and went to the duty-free to buy some liquor for some Chinese friends. He boarded the plane at 9:45 a.m. The plane took off at 10:00 a.m. When Adam arrived in Beijing after a 14-hour flight, he went through Immigration and Customs. He took a taxi to his hotel. He went straight to bed because he was very tired.

3. What is the talk mainly about?

(A) The reason why Adam decided to fly to China

(B) Some friends Adam was going to meet in China

(C) A tiring day for Adam

(D) A flying experience for Adam

【Day 5】
Friday

4. Which of the following statements about Adam is "NOT" true?

(A) He was late for the plane.

(B) He did some shopping at the airport.

(C) A cab drove him to the hotel.

(D) He has some Chinese friends.

5. What might be the time when Adam went through customs?

   (A) 9 a.m.

   (B) 10:45 a.m.

   (C) 12 a.m.

   (D) 12:45 a.m.

Questions 6 to 9 refer to the following talk.

Kevin's career came out of a legendary experience. He left school when he was 17 and took a job as a pizza deliverer. The pay was low so Kevin tried to find another part time job to make extra money. However, life was just not easy for him. He couldn't find any payment elsewhere except the pizzeria. Fortunately, the chef decided to teach him how to make pizza. He learned very well. Five years later, he was a qualified sous chef. In the first year in his new job, he met Samantha, who worked in the pizzeria as a waitress. She was two years younger than Kevin and was tall and slim with shoulder length blond hair. Five months later, they got married. At the wedding Kevin met Samantha's teenage brother. He happened to be a waiter from a diner. The three formed a group and started their own mobile pizzeria. Friends told them that their food was very good and that they ought to think of running their own pizzeria chain. They are now doing very well as a franchise pizzeria holder.

6. What can be inferred from the talk?

   (A) Samantha's brother is younger than Kevin.

   (B) Kevin had a good time working in a café.

   (C) Samantha and David formed a group before marriage.

   (D) Kevin got a part-time job when he decided to run a business.

7. What is NOT true about Samantha?

   (A) She has long black hair.

   (B) She was 20 when she got married.

   (C) She worked as a waitress.

   (D) She is tall and slim.

8. How many jobs has Kevin had since he was 17?

   (A) 4

   (B) 3

   (C) 2

   (D) 1

9. Which food does the group probably "NOT" serve?

   (A) Bread

   (B) Pizza

   (C) Sushi

   (D) Chicken wings

MP3 072

Expanded talks

1.

Morgan Stason has a happy family. They live in Taipei. He is an English teacher from Canada, and married to a Taiwanese woman, Miranda. She is an owner of a Cram school. They make a great career together in Taipei city. They have two children. Their names are Teddy and Maggie. They live in Taipei County and drive about one hour to the cram school every day. The children go to the primary school near where their parents work.

MP3 073

2.

On June 2nd, we started the day bright and early by the Hiking at Jade State Park. By 8:00 am we passed the Entry to the state park. After rounding up backpacks filled with water bottles, snacks, sun-block, bug repellent, band-aids, and the camera, we got ready for a day of fun. We planned to hike the 290 acre Jade Lake with 22 miles of trails. They are beautiful paths that weave through forests and open meadows. We wore lightweight pants to protect our legs from brambles and poison ivy. About 12:30, at the end of our hike, there is the boat launch area. We wandered close to the water's edge to skip rocks and toss pebbles. Then, for the rest of the day, we spread blankets on shaded lawn areas for picnic tables and enjoyed a peaceful view of Jade Lake under the shade of many trees with a cooling breeze off the lake. Around 4:00 pm, we had to leave the paradise reluctantly before the sun set. By the time we got home, we were all exhausted with fully loaded memories and went to have a sweet dream with smiles.

MP3 074

3.

Wu Pao Chun was brought up by a poor family of eight children, and lost his father at the age of 12. He left home at 17 to Taipei and became a bread apprentice. The life of an apprentice was even harder than his childhood. He was hurt by the burning tray in the arms all the time. Finally, after 4 years of hard work, he made a traditional baker. However, the traditional baking was outdated in the market, and Wu's bread was in serious decline in the sales.

At that time, Wu sought comments from a famous self-taught baker, Chen Fu-guang. Chen taught him to cast aside the conventional baking, and redefines the word "delicious", which is the taste of red wine, cheese, French cuisine, and delicacies.

With Chen's help, Wu broadened his horizons and even started to learn Japanese in order to read foreign recipes.

Encouraged by friends and business partners, Wu began his working career in 2005. He eventually took part in bakery competitions in Taiwan. His home-grown leaven became his secret weapon. In 2007, he won the Asian bakery championship. The following year, Wu and two other fellow bakers from Taiwan won silver medals in the bread Olympiad's in Paris, France. Wu also won the individual European bread winner. In 2010, Wu represented Taiwan to participate in the inaugural World Cup in Paris Masters Bread, defeated the other seven country participants, and further won the European-style bread group world champion.

MP3 075

I use the Internet every day. With the Internet, I can access desired information instantly. I can find out what's happening around the world in just a few minutes, and I can also get in touch with friends through e-mail, and they can get back to me very quickly in just a few minutes. With the invention of the Internet, the distance between people is less than it used to be. But there are some problems as well. People sometimes post violent or pornographic pictures on the Internet. Young children, who like to browse the Internet, are very likely to see them. In addition, gangsters can use the Internet to buy and sell weapons and drugs without getting caught. These are problems we are not really happy when we see them. Improper uses of the Internet have led to more problems than we can think of. Sometimes these problems are too crippled to cope.

Expanded answer
MP3 076

There are both advantages and disadvantages in the Internet. The benefits are:

First, it has the most information resources accessible on almost all subjects, ranging from government law and services, trade fairs and conferences, market information, new innovations and technical support, resources for homework, medicine, to even advice on personal affairs.

Second, it provides the best and fastest communication.

Third, it has real-time communication with someone in another part of the world and video conferencing, chat, and messenger services all over the world.

Fourth, it has online services and E-commerce, such as booking tickets for a movie, transferring funds, paying utility bills and taxes without leaving our homes or offices, and it has E-commerce transferring money through the Internet, reaching over a variety of products and services, such as eBay. It also has Wikipedia, Coursera, Babbel, Archive, and Teachertube, sharing knowledge with people of all age groups.

Fifth, it has entertainment for everyone to find the latest updates about celebrities and exploring lifestyle websites and downloading games either for a price or for free.

Sixth, it has social networks, such as Facebook or Twitter staying connected with friends and family, get in touch with the latest happenings in the world and has networks searching and applying for jobs and business opportunities on forums and communities. It also has chat rooms to meet new people.

Seventh, it has inexhaustible education, the World Wide Web (WWW) from the academic, to greater knowledge and know-how on subjects making it possible of homeschooling with videos of teachers just like in a real classroom.

MP3 077

The problems of the internet:

First, our online personal information for banking, social networking, or other services, is often stolen or misused by thieving websites and individuals causing the problems by having our identities misused and our accounts been broken into.

Second, our computer system may be slowed down by spam e-mails serving endless lines of advertisements the mixing with our more important emails. Third, our system is attacked and completely crashed by virus programs activated simply by clicking a seemingly harmless link. Fourth, our children are exposed to adult content as age-inappropriate pornography as the biggest problem of the Internet, lacking of control over the distribution to. Fifth, excessive surfing, online gambling, and social networking create both physical and mental health complications resulting in social isolation, obesity, and depression.

MP3 078

I think in the long run, the gap between the rich and poor will become more obvious. Although the measurement of this gap is lower than the international warning line, the survey of family income, we found the gap will be widened in the future.

Causes of the wealth gap associated with globalization, which made financial liberalization, information communication technology progress, trade barriers reduction, the deepening integration of the global economy, the release of the labor force in emerging economies. Besides, in light of technical progress and wage equalization, the low-skilled and unskilled labor tends to be unemployed in the higher technical developed countries, and caused a wage compression. In particular, Taiwan's the main production model, the acting industry or OEM (original equipment manufacturer), made meager profits, repress unskilled workers' wages and expand the uneven distribution of income.

Expanded talk

MP3 079

After the financial tsunami, funds loose fueled a speculative bubble. Low interest rates, loose monetary environment, resulted in real estate prices and the impact of low-income families. In addition, long-term tax policy tilted to the rich. Tax cuts continued to capitalists, such as the inheritance and gift tax in 2009. Foreign assets were remitted back to Taiwan speculation in real estate, while not importing into the substantial investment to increase employment opportunities worsening a polarization gap. Moreover, public resources are unevenly distributed. More resources are given to the north rather than the south, resulting in a long-term uneven land development. Therefore, the south is suffering from income inequality problems.

MP3 080

Part 1

Question and Answer

Q：They all think the death penalty is worse than a life sentence. Which do you think is worse?

A：I think/believe a life sentence is worse.

Q：Would you prefer traveling abroad or in your homeland?

A：I would prefer traveling abroad.

Q：Would you rather swim indoors or outdoors?

A：I would rather swim outdoors.

Q：People usually would eat out on the weekend. Do you agree or disagree?

A: I agree that eating on the weekend is good for the family reunion.

Q: It has recently been announced that a project is to be built. Would you support or oppose the project?

A: I would oppose because the project that will hinder the transportation.

Q: What is your opinion on raising tax on the rich?

A: My opinion is raising tax on the rich would help narrow the gap of incomes.

Q: If you can make an important decision on charging or not charging the U-bike in the first half hour, which would you do?

A: If I could make a decision, I would charge the U-bike.

Q: Are you in favor of the school/community's doing?

A: I am in favor of the school's policy.

MP3 081

Part 2

1. Would you prefer to <u>travel</u> in your homeland or <u>abroad</u>?
   Answer: I think I would prefer to <u>travel abroad</u>.

2. Do you agree or disagree that boys learn better in science than girls do?
   Answer: I disagree <u>boys learn better in science than girls</u>.

3. The municipality will use part of your community as a depot of the refuse truck. Do you support or oppose the plan?

Answer: I would oppose the plan to use part of my community as a depot of the refuse truck.

MP3 082

Part 3 Listing

First, second, third..., First of all, The first reason is, The second reason is, The other reason is, Another reason why it is, The final reason is, Also, I also think that, etc.

MP3 083

Part 4

Would you prefer to study abroad or in your own country?

Answer:

Topic

I would prefer to study in my own country.

Supporting points

The first reason is I would have many troubles with the language.

Also, I can't get used to the foreign customs.

The final reason is, I couldn't stand with the homesickness when I am alone.

MP3 084

Question 11:

Express an Opinion: In this part of the test, you will give your opinion about a specific topic. Be sure to say as much as you can in the time allowed. You will have 15 seconds to prepare. Then you will have 60 seconds to speak. Do you agree or disagree with the following statement?

Is it better to purchase things on websites rather than through ordinary shops?

Use specific reasons and examples to support your answer.

MP3 085

Answer 1

I think that it is better to purchase things on the website rather than the ordinary shops.

First, incredible convenience: traditional stores operate with fixed hours, while online shoppers can choose any time of the day or night to get on the Web and shop. This is especially convenient for families with small children, or simply in bad weather. Second, price comparisons: you don't have to walk all day "in the market for" the best deal when you visit a website to settle for whatever price the site has placed on a particular item. Third, limitless choice: shelf space in a traditional store is limited, while on line you can find as various goods as you like. Fourth, no pressure sales: eager salespeople bug you all the time in a real market but you don't have to put up with that online.

MP3 086

Answer 2

I don't like buying goods online.

The first reason is: you can't have a feel about clothes you'd like to purchase. You really need to see how it's made when purchasing a cloth. Even if you are familiar with a certain brand, you can also buy a cloth that's not suitable for you. Sometimes the return policy and shipment are annoying. If you're buying a clothing item, it's impossible to feel the material and see how it's made. Unless you know your sizes and are familiar with the brand of selling clothing, this could end up being a bad experience.

Another reason is that you can't ask someone about the products immediately. If you have a question about the item, you probably will have to wait at least 24 hours to get a question answered.

I am also concerned about privacy and security: privacy and security are desperate concerns for any online shopper. For that misgiving, you need to make sure your transaction is a safe one, install free spyware removal tools, identify online scams and hoaxes, surf anonymously, and keep your Web usage private.

【Day 3】
Wednesday

MP3 087

Listen and repeat

There are many ways to do this, but I think...

Maybe most people would agree with this but I...

Most of the opinions are in favor of that decision, but if I had a choice, I guess I would say...

Well it's a hard question, but I think the most important thing is...

I think there are pros and cons for this issue, but if I had to choose, I would say...

MP3 088

Listen and repeat

1. Some students prefer to live outside of campus, near the downtown, shops, restaurants, or entertainments. Other students maintain living in the dormitory where it is quiet and convenient for any study facilities. Which one do you prefer and why?

2. Some people think teenagers should be taught at school on how to raise children of their own, others think that it is their parent's duty to teach them. What is your opinion and why?

MP3 089

Listen and repeat

1. There are many pros and cons for living in or out of the campus but if I had to choose, I would prefer to live out of the campus where I can temporarily stay out of the anxious academic atmosphere as well. My parents like most of the others, are for the campus side though.

2. There are many things that teenagers are taught to equip themselves with their life, and raising children is one of them. My opinion is that schools should be responsible for teaching the teenagers some necessary skills of raising children. The main reason is that parents are too busy to supervise their children to do their homework, let alone their own business. The other reason is that nowadays to many parents' surprise, more and more teenagers get pregnant, and they are totally unprepared for the emergency, let alone thinking of teaching them how to raise the baby.

MP3 090

(Listen and repeat)

<u>In my experience</u>, it is better to major in a subject I like because it is more important to feel happy than to be a student from a famous school.

<u>To me,</u> regular exercise is really important because it helps you stay fit.

The main reason why I think the campus shouldn't be a depot of the refuse trucks is that the foul smell they emit affects the teachers and students.

It did happen to me before, and in that case I chose not to tell parents immediately about their children's misbehavior and helped them to tell their parents themselves.

In my family, the problem was serious once, so I have a good experience to deal with it.

....

MP3 091

Some people think it is better to buy groceries on sale, others prefer to buy them at an ordinary price. What is your opinion on purchase timing?

(Listen and repeat)

To me, buying on sale is always disappointing because we tend to buy too many unnecessary things.

The main reason I think for not buying things on sale is that you might buy too many things you don't really need.

It did happen to me before, and in that case I chose not to buy anything on sale for things were mostly at the end of expiry date.

In my family, we don't buy groceries on sale as the market or shopping mall is always crowded and children are overwhelmed by the fatigue and are struggling with the crowds.

In my experience, buying groceries on sale is the stupidest

thing in life. When we buy a lot of cheap, unnecessary things appearing to be some "trophies" in a battle of rush, we simply spend more money than we try to save.

MP3 092

Question one

Should college students take on a part time job? Why or why not?

Answers to question one

(Listen and repeat)

1. I don't agree with the statement college students should take part time jobs.
2. They need to focus on their own academic task, and part time jobs occupy too much time. Part time jobs may consume too much of their energy before they can practice any theories they have learned.
3. Part time jobs help college students apply their theories on practice.
4. I don't think about if college students should take on part time jobs.

MP3 093

Question two

Do you prefer shopping in a traditional market or a supermarket? Why?

Answers to question two

(Listen and repeat)

1. I prefer shopping in a supermarket.
2. Supermarket is cleaner. Traditional market is usually wet and nasty with butchering chicken and fish. Supermarket's prices are all fixed. Tricky bargain in traditional market bothers me.
3. Traditional market offers good social occasions for shoppers and venders.
4. I prefer shopping in a supermarket.

MP3 094

Listen and repeat

I prefer fast walking to jogging.

= I prefer to walk fast rather than jog.

= I prefer to walk fast instead of jogging

MP3 095

I would rather shop online than go to the market.

The children would swim there rather than sail a bamboo raft.

MP3 096

Not that I love Caesar less, but that I love Rome more.

Some praise him, whereas others condemn him.

Hospitals in the south tend to be better equipped, while those in the north are relatively poor.

Although they're expensive, they last forever and never go out of style.

MP3 097

I don't eat much, yet I weigh 90 kg.

Some of the students failed. However, all the girls did quite well.

There was still a long way to go. Nonetheless, some progress had been made.

The news may be unexpected; nevertheless, it has been confirmed.

On the one hand, the low oil price makes consumers happy. On the other hand, if it remains low, the macro economy may be harmed.

People all say they don't do things like that. On the contrary, they do them all the time.

Answers to question one

MP3 098

(Listen and repeat)

Most people encourage college students to take on part time jobs, but I don't think college students should take part time jobs because they need to focus on their own academic task, and part time jobs occupy too much of their time. However, some people maintain that part time jobs help college students apply their theories to practice. Yet, part time jobs may consume too much of their energy before they can practice any theories they have learned. Therefore, I still don't agree with college students taking on part time jobs.

Answers to question two
MP3 099
(Listen and repeat)

I prefer shopping in a supermarket because supermarket is cleaner. Nevertheless, traditional market offers good social occasions for shoppers and venders; but to me, traditional market butchering chicken and fish is usually wet and nasty. Although bargaining in traditional market gives a kind of pleasure, bargain is still tricky and bothers me. I would definitely prefer shopping in the supermarket.

MP3 100

Question 1

Due to a recent air crash in the middle of the city, public opinion is shifting. People are in favor of moving the airport. Do you support or oppose the opinion? Why?

Answer

I would support the opinion to move the airport away from the center of the city.

First of all, with the recent accident as a warning sign, the frequent ascent and descent of the aircraft poses a potential threat to citizens' life. Also, while the city is developing with a more and more population, some residents inevitably suffer from a huge noise. As the urban development grows, the large amount of land an airport requires becomes a barrier space to progressing constructions.

On the other hand, one of the biggest benefits of erecting the airport in the center of a city is the convenience. People living near the airport have enjoyed the convenience and profits they bring. Also, this has opened more business opportunities for businessmen and the pleasure for travelers. After all, the city has the nature of transportation center which makes the best use of an airport. Meanwhile, it is a big business and would create lots of jobs for local people.

That being said, I would still prefer to travel further to an airport than to have one close to my house.

MP3 101

Question 2

Some people admire innovation, and they take up a challenge against the tradition. Others like to stay with routines and don't want to make any change. Which attitude do you prefer? Explain your reason.

Answer

I would adopt an attitude of innovation and new ways of life.

Innovation brings us new ways of doing things, building things and new ideas to change the world we got used to, so being innovative involves challenges and risks defying the tradition. Challenge broadens our horizon of reality improving our present life. Challenging the tradition allows people to develop different talents and has created a better world. For example, Bill Gates dropped out of Harvard for the more innovative Microsoft. This has not only created his outstanding technology career, but also introduced a brand new information world for human beings. Quitting Harvard must be the hardest choice to make for any student, but Gate's courage of taking that step eventually paid off.

On the other hand, we like opportunities under guaranteed security that comes with knowing what will happen. Following the routines of Harvard, Gates could easily find a steady job after graduation. Betting ones most promising education on a risky business is the last decision for most of us to make.

Having said that, I would prefer to have some adventure just like what Bill Gates had, so I would adopt an innovative attitude to life.

英語學習 ─職場系列─

定價：NT$349元/HK$109元
規格：320頁/17＊23cm

定價：NT$360元/HK$113元
規格：328頁/17＊23cm

定價：NT$349元/HK$109元
規格：304頁/17＊23cm

定價：NT$360元/HK$113元
規格：320頁/17＊23cm

定價：NT$369元/HK$115元
規格：312頁/17＊23cm/MP3

定價：NT$369元/HK$115元
規格：320頁/17＊23cm

定價：NT$360元/HK$113元
規格：288頁/17＊23cm/MP3

定價：NT$329元/HK$103元
規格：304頁/17＊23cm

定價：NT$369元/HK$115元
規格：328頁/17＊23cm/MP3

英語學習 —生活・文法・考用—

定價：NT$369元/K$115元
規格：320頁/17＊23cm/MP3

定價：NT$380元/HK$119元
規格：320頁/17＊23cm/MP3

定價：NT$349元/HK$109元
規格：352頁/17＊23cm

定價：NT$380元/HK$119元
規格：288頁/17＊23cm/MP3

定價：NT$329元/HK$103元
規格：352頁/17＊23cm

定價：NT$349元/HK$109元
規格：304頁/17＊23cm

定價：NT$380元/HK$119元
規格：352頁/17＊23cm

定價：NT$369元/HK$115元
規格：304頁/17＊23cm/MP3

定價：NT$380元/HK$119元
規格：304頁/17＊23cm/MP3

Leader 019

一學就會的英檢口說高分術：　10-60 歲都適用的四週英語口說課!!

作　　者　常安陸
封面構成　高鍾琪
內頁構成　華漢電腦排版有限公司

發 行 人　周瑞德
企劃編輯　劉俞青
執行編輯　陳韋佑
校　　對　陳欣慧、饒美君
印　　製　大亞彩色印刷製版股份有限公司
初　　版　2015 年 5 月
定　　價　新台幣 380 元
出　　版　力得文化
電　　話　(02) 2351-2007
傳　　真　(02) 2351-0887
地　　址　100 台北市中正區福州街 1 號 10 樓之 2
E - m a i l　best.books.service@gmail.com

港澳地區總經銷　泛華發行代理有限公司
地　　　　址　香港新界將軍澳工業邨駿昌街 7 號 2 樓
電　　　　話　(852) 2798-2323
傳　　　　真　(852) 2796-5471

國家圖書館出版品預行編目(CIP)資料

　一學就會的英檢口說高分術 ：
10-60 歲都適用的四週英語口說
課! / 常安陸著. -- 初版. --
臺北市 ： 力得文化, 2015.05
面 ；　公分. -- (Leader ；19)
ISBN 978-986-91458-7-9(平裝)
1.英語 2.會話
805.1892　　104006372